Ben

Dead Dungeon Book Four

S Mays

Beneath the Dungeon

Dead Dungeon Book Four

S Mays

Mailing List[1]

Facebook[2]

Website[3]

Cover art by: Alberto Besi

Cover typography: Plumstone Book Covers

V-F03112020

---

1. https://www.subscribepage.com/SMaysSuperbTales

2. http://www.facebook.com/superbtales

3. http://www.s-mays.com

Dedication

For Gimmy, Gaston, Luke, and Whiskers.

Other Books by S Mays

https://www.s-mays.com/the-good-stuff.html

Please leave a review! They help authors tremendously!

CHAPTER ONE
New Rule

The consortium gathered in my throne room was more motley than any creatures that inhabited my dungeon. The group was comprised of several guild leaders, noblemen, and the heads of the church. They were understandably upset.

"You do not have the authority to steal our profits and wealth! If the kingdom requires more tax revenue, then raise taxes on the peasants!" a young man dressed in red regal finery shouted. The others in attendance nodded and grumbled in agreement.

"Your father had an ironclad contract with us. You can't change it!" a priest dressed in Uxper's robes complained. "You must release the members of our clergy you have imprisoned. They have done nothing wrong according to the law!"

One by one, they yelled out their grievances. Slumped on my throne, I listened for another hour as the richest and most powerful people in Tharune complained that they did not have enough wealth and power. Once their grumbling finally died down, I stood.

"Thank you for expressing your concerns with me. I'll consider your words carefully. Please follow the attendant, who will lead you back to the surface... and please don't stray from the path. The last nobleman who did so ended up transformed into a ghoul."

"We came here for answers! We won't be leaving until you tell us of your plans!" the young nobleman in red shouted. "You cannot simply steal half our wealth!"

"Xagrim."

Upon seeing the death knight moving toward them, the majority of the crowd began shuffling toward the exit.

The death knight marched toward the lone nobleman and stood silently. The man shifted uneasily but refused to budge. Xagrim slowly looked down at the man as his eyes glowed. "Do you challenge the Master?" he asked in a deep, hollow tone that sounded more like an accusation rather than a question.

The group quickened their pace as they exited, leaving the angry protester to fend for himself. The young man glanced at his fleeing compatriots then back to the knight before dashing out of the throne room. Xagrim moved back to his position at the bottom of the steps that led up to my throne.

"I've faced many dangers since coming to this dungeon, but none I dread more than these meetings with these pompous elite bastards," I said.

Zarah appeared beside me, dressed in an outfit that was similar to those worn by the royal accountants. It seemed she relished her new role as an assistant to the king. Unrolling a long parchment, she marked off the latest event. "You have one more meeting today, and then you're scheduled to train with Leath. Oh, and your shipment of books just came in."

Books...I hadn't had time to finish a single one since becoming king. Now I had not just a dungeon to maintain, but an entire kingdom. At one point before all of this, I'd thought I'd go mad from boredom. Now I savored the idea of a day with nothing to do. Why did it always seem when your wish was granted, the results were worse than your situation before?

"Are you listening?" Zarah asked.

I hadn't been aware she'd kept talking. "I think I've had enough for today. Cancel the meeting with...whoever it was," I said as I stood and stretched.

"But it's the head of the Merchant Guild. He's been waiting all day! He's threatening to leave the city!"

"He can wait the night, too," I said as I descended the steps. As I exited the throne room, a smiling rotund man and his assistants rushed to greet me. I waved them away as Zarah stepped in to talk to him. "Everyone must leave. Now!" I shouted. Most of the rabble were already gone, but a few had lingered in the Dire Hall. They began to file out.

"Does that include me, Your Highness?" Leath asked.

I smiled. "Of course not. We have a sparring session. As soon as the blood begins to flow to my lower extremities again, we can begin." The Master of the Guard saluted me, but I reached out and grasped his hand.

Leath used a standard longsword while I wielded Purgatory. His enchanted blade, Galvas, would easily damage my unenchanted weapon, so he opted for the ordinary blade. Zhalix had repaired the damage from our fight with Leath's group of powerful adventurers, but she had let me hear her discontent over the matter.

"How are things in the city?" I asked as I lunged forward.

"Oh, you mean after half of the guild leaders and upper crust fled the city once they heard what you planned?" Leath said as he deflected the strike. "More have fled since then."

"I mean, have you found the rest of my family?" Although I had to admit — I found the news that even more of the aristocracy and city leaders were gone to be depressing.

"I suspect they were ushered to safety once the goblins poured into the castle and kidnapped the king. The last I heard, they traveled to the Merromont estate along with the others."

I leapt back from an attack he'd aimed at my lower legs. "I'm surprised the Merromonts are offering them sanctuary. Our forces would crush theirs."

"Yes, well, about that..."

I paused our combat. "We've lost more soldiers?"

"At least three hundred more. I believe the fleeing members of the guilds and the church bribed them to defect."

At this rate, New Vadis might end up abandoned. "I thought you'd stationed the Royal Guard to keep any more from leaving?"

"These people have hidey holes throughout the city. Sewer tunnels, teleportation stones. They were all prepared to protect their wealth from attack or intrusion, son. Seems they didn't exactly trust your father, either."

"A new king scares them so much that they'd abandon their guild houses, workers, and factories?" I asked.

"A new king whose first orders were to imprison the heads of the church, and who asked for business ledgers concerning all slave trade and newly minted illegal activities so that he could lock up the business leaders does, yes. What did you think would happen, Jagen?"

"I expected them to obey their king."

Leath shook his head. "You may be a prodigy at combat and magic, but you know so little of matters of state. You must be diplomatic with these people. Locking them away and torturing them will turn the rest against you."

"I want security around the city doubled. No more people are allowed to leave for the next few days. Once they see what I have planned, they will change their minds," I said.

Leath slid his sword into his scabbard. "I think you're making a big mistake, son. You can't treat a city like your dungeon. If they want to leave, let them. It will only go badly if you keep the dissenters locked up with the others. They'll turn them all against you."

I sheathed Purgatory. "I understand, but we must stem the exodus. If too many leave, the city will collapse completely."

"I'll see what I can do. We're lucky riots haven't started yet, Jagen."

"Yes...we are. You're needed more in the city than here. I'd like to set up some sort of communication service if possible so that you won't be forced to travel to the dungeon to see me. Are there any master wizards left?"

"What do you think? I put in your request, but none have answered. I believe many of the guild artisans and adventurers have fled as well. Executing Archbishop Phell and Elemental Lord Yolune didn't do you any favors with the guilds. I'll head back and redouble our efforts," he said as he turned to leave.

I grasped my mentor's shoulder. "I appreciate your loyalty and...even more, your guidance and friendship."

"And I appreciate your faith in me, Jagen. I'll do my best," Leath said as he placed his hand on my shoulder. "I feel as if we are balanced upon the edge of a blade, and the next few weeks will determine not just our fates, but the fate of the city and perhaps the kingdom." He turned and left.

Things weren't going as I'd planned. While I had expected the plutocrats to rebel, I hadn't been worried since the Royal Guard and Army were at my disposal. I hadn't predicted the populace would side against me out of fear.

To make matters worse, my requests to parlay with the Nosterans' king, Aiyla's father, hadn't been received well. I'd hoped that with Tharune under my control, we could finally broker peace between our two countries, but it seemed he blamed me for Aiyla's death. Perhaps he even believed I had manipulated her into leaving the safety of his city in order to murder her. I would not stop until the war ended. It was my last promise to Aiyla before I returned home from our wedding.

A goblin tentatively approached and waited patiently until I motioned for him to speak.

"Goblins wonder when go home. Magic stone not work. Master said he fix."

I'd almost forgotten the teleportation stone had been damaged by the last attack on the dungeon. Half of the torture devices were destroyed, along with much of the goblin level's furniture and a third of the church. Drundt had been overseeing the reconstruction, but he couldn't repair magical devices like the teleporter, or some of the magical implements of torture.

"Zarah," I called out.

"An enchanter should arrive soon. There were...problems," she said as she appeared to the side and checked her phantasmal list.

"What sort of...never mind. I don't want to know. As long as we finally have one, I'm satisfied. We have enough work to keep him or her busy for months. Is everything ready for the enchanter's arrival?"

"The shipment of common enchanting reagents arrived yesterday. I had them delivered to the artisan level."

We returned to my bedroom, where I stripped and showered. After dressing, I took a seat at my desk, burying my head in my hands.

"Is something wrong?" Zarah asked.

"I...didn't know it would be this difficult. I feel like the kingdom's slipping through my fingers. If I were there, perhaps things could be different. The people need to see their leader, not his emissaries. When Leath visits me to receive my instructions, it takes him away from his duties. While the people trust him, they are being fed lies about me from the plutocrats while Leath is gone."

"I told you that there was no way you could rule the kingdom and the dungeon."

"Yes, you did. I'm still going to attempt it. I simply need trusted people in power. Even my father couldn't do it alone."

She grew pensive at the mention of the previous king.

"What is it?"

"You were finally reunited with your father..."

Again with this argument. I was patient with her because, for much of her life, all she wanted was to have her family back. "Reunited? You make it seem as if I missed him. I had no memories of him, other than his killing of Aiyla. He received a just punishment. A quick death was too good for him."

"But...your own father?"

"My father was not like yours, Zarah. You said your father was a good, loving man. One that sacrificed for his family and brought hope into the world. My father cared only for power and wealth. If not for people like him, your family might have lived. You might have been happy. Sometimes we must sacrifice the ones closest to us for the betterment of all."

A jimp appeared in the doorway, carrying several covered dishes on a tray. At least that would end the debate. "Finally, dinner is served," I said as I motioned for him to set it on the desk.

Ho'Scar still found the time to prepare my meals even with his torture chamber and cells full. We'd even resorted to keeping some of the prisoners in the jail, watched over by the skeletons. We hadn't had a single group enter the dungeon since Leath's.

I supposed the guilds didn't want to risk the ire of the king until things had settled down. That worried me, as the dungeon depended on a regular supply of adventurers, but at the moment we had more than enough prisoners from the corrupt guards, aristocracy, brigands, and church officials.

Serving as both the king and master of the dungeon could prove impossible, just as Zarah had warned. We now held some valuable artifacts and other treasure we'd confiscated from the Uxper Orthodoxy as well as the kingdom's treasury. While I left the bulk of the wealth in the city, I'd made it clear that we'd moved some to the dungeon. We should have been very busy with interlopers and adventurers, but we'd seen none. Perhaps they were planning and scheming to raid us at some future point.

"Aren't you forgetting something?" Zarah asked as I dipped my spoon into the bowl of stew. She nodded toward my meal.

"Ah, yes," I said as I held out my utensil. Toxin slipped out of the shadows and sniffed it before placing it into his mouth. He spat the remnants into his hand. "Poisoned."

I threw up my hands in frustration. Another meal ruined. "That's the third time. How are they intercepting the food between Ho'Scar and myself?"

"You have dozens of visitors every day. I can't watch them all every second they are here. Groups are coming and going on every level. All it would take is one talented rogue or perhaps a summoned creature to slip through."

"I can't simply ban these people from the dungeon. I feel as if I'm making at least a little progress with some of the guilds."

"Like you said, you can't do it all alone. You need some trusted advisers within the bureaucracy."

"Aside from Leath, I have no one. He wasn't exactly entrenched within the inner workings of my father's empire for the past few years. I'm an outsider, without knowledge of the ties that bind these powers to each other. The two of us are ill-suited to endear support from the aristocracy."

"Leath doesn't have connections?"

"No. My mentor had no desire for power or position. Battle and adoration are all he cared for. I'm afraid that while he wields power through my permission, he won't know how to direct it."

"Perhaps you should find allies who know the inner workings of the city."

"Yes, I've attempted to ascertain who would be most beneficial to me, but the ones in power are loath to share that power or submit to mine. It seems my father was for sale to the highest bidder, and my reputation as a reformer has shut those doors to me. How would I find out who the powerful people in the city were?"

Zarah asked, "Why not ask them?"

"I don't believe they will be forthcoming with information that will help me destroy their base of power."

"I didn't say you should ask nicely..."

CHAPTER TWO
Farewells

The torture chamber looked almost as good as new. With the help of the artisans as well as skilled workers I'd hired from the guilds, it hadn't taken long to rebuild the devious devices and repair the damage the group of master adventurers had done to the room. Of course, some of the devices were enchanted and would need specific magics to function properly. Strangely enough, most of those had survived the fight and the ensuing fire. Perhaps there were also enchantments upon them that improved their durability. I had no time to investigate the matter, but perhaps in the future...

Ho'Scar looked up from his workbench, where he was tinkering with a set of gears. "Master, I done got that information ya asked for." He seemed to be in an elated mood. Looking around the room, I could see why.

Half of the torture devices contained prisoners. Moans or muffled protests erupted as we proceeded across the room. The torture business was booming at the moment, and Ho'Scar couldn't have been more pleased.

"Here's the list 'o people you wanted. I got 'em to rat each other out, just in case they weren't too honest about it. Turns out some of the ones we thought were high-level guild members or clergy were just imposters forced ta take the fall fer their masters."

I felt my temperature rise as I snatched the list from the pig-man. "What do you mean, many of them are imposters?" As I perused the list, my anger grew. I thought we'd captured five high-ranking members of the plutocracy, but the most prestigious prisoner was only a bishop within the Uxper Orthodoxy.

"How could this have happened?" I asked, trying to keep my voice calm.

"I guess they brought us the wrong people?" Ho'Scar offered.

I glared at him. "Of course they did! This was intentional. They must have arranged it so the guards were paid to arrest scapegoats and patsies. I'd assumed we had at least a few people of worth. Without my memories, I wouldn't know who the leaders of these organizations are, and Leath is blissfully ignorant of such things, as he never attended events related to matters of state."

"What now?" Zarah asked as she appeared behind Ho'Scar.

I thought on the matter. The people we had imprisoned would likely know who their superiors were, but much of the aristocracy and clergy had fled the city. These scapegoats had provided time for their masters to escape. While the number of people fleeing had concerned me, I had assumed it was mostly a combination of the plutocracy and the peasants, but now it seemed we'd lost a great deal of the very people we wanted to punish. Only the ones who had been too slow or who had been our first targets had been unlucky enough to be caught in our net. Many had left behind a portion of their wealth, homes, and estates. We'd been happy to confiscate the remnants, but most contained nothing of value other than the buildings and land itself. I should have secretly raided their homes before announcing my ascension to the throne, but such a move smacked of the very authoritarianism I wanted to combat. By formally announcing the change in rule, it had given them time to plan their escapes.

"We need strong leadership to take the place of ones who fled. I need to know the structures of these guilds, the churches, and the noble houses. Find out what these people know, and we will begin constructing charts so we will know who and what is missing," I said.

"Leath said much of the castle staff remained captured after your assault. Surely some of them would know these things?" Zarah offered.

I smiled. "Some were members of the Royal Tax Collection Agency. I hadn't thought of that. They will have detailed reports on these organizations, including the positions and titles of the members, the number of workers, and how much they are paid. It's ironic such a mundane agency would have so much information at its disposal. The bureaucracy may have much of the missing information we need."

"Never overlook the quill-pushers," Zarah said as she nodded in agreement.

"So, um, what do ya want me to do with these guys?" Ho'Scar said.

"Continue gathering information. Provide Zarah with any facts you can squeeze out of them," I said as I turned to leave. "And don't become too overzealous. Without a steady supply of adventurers, we depend on the trickle of magic from these prisoners to maintain the Soul Sphere," I shouted over my shoulder. I didn't want to return to the days where we fretted over dwindling magical reserves.

ENCHANTING WAS A RARE discipline that required years of intense study. In addition, only a select few were adept enough to make a living at it. The lesser ones were relegated to employment in workshops, creating magical orbs of light, firesparkers, minor enchanted bags, and other knickknacks. The enchanter that finally showed up seemed to be barely a step up from those workers.

"P-Publin Chaosun," the young man stammered as he approached my throne.

"You are the enchanter I sent for?" I asked. The thin, dark-haired young man looked to be in his early twenties. Bony and ashen, he seemed to shun the sun more than I did. He couldn't have advanced far in his studies. This was the best enchanter the King of Tharune was offered by the guilds? It was an intentional affront.

"I-I'm sorry, Your Majesty. I was the only one w-who answered the job posted on the guild message board," the young man stammered. He was practically trembling.

I lowered my voice to ease his concern. "I appreciate your assistance, Publin. I was merely expecting someone more...advanced."

"I-I'm sorry, Your Majesty. I wasn't made aware the j-job had a skill requirement. I merely saw there was a lot of work to be done, and I n-need experience. I'm just l-looking for work and a chance to prove myself."

I smiled. "Work is something we have an abundance of. Tell me — are you able to cast high-level enchantments?"

The young spellcaster looked around the room nervously. "I-I've had some success with third level enchantments, and I'm fairly skilled with second level."

It was as I suspected. He must have graduated within the past year, if at all. He must have noticed the look of disappointment because he spoke up before I could comment on his lack of experience.

"B-but I graduated third in my class, and I'm a fast learner. I just...really need this. I'm sorry. Most of the shops in the city aren't hiring or closed up recently due to the...turmoil."

"I'm not sure you are what —" I began, but Zarah's soft voice whispered in my ear.

"Give the poor fellow a break. He'll be more loyal than a high-ranking guild member. We don't need advanced enchantments on everything right now, and he can learn. If he proves too incompetent, you can hand him over to Ho'Scar."

"Very well. My...assistant will see to your contract. I'll see that the proper enchanting materials are delivered to your room, which will be on the floor above this one. Zarah will explain compensation, meals, and other mundane details."

"A-above?" Publin asked as he looked up at the ceiling, as if expecting demons to descend upon him. "I didn't know I'd have to live in the dungeon."

"I have several artisans currently living here. You may learn something from them if you seek them out. It's not permanent. Once your work is completed, you will leave. Unless you would *like* to stay and become a permanent member of the dungeon?"

His eyes grew wide with fright. "N-no! I'm happy with the agreement. Thank you, Dungeon Mas — King Therion! Thank you for this chance. I won't disappoint you!"

My voice grew stern as I leaned over and looked down at him from my throne. "See that you don't, Novice Chaosun."

He backed away, bowing as he went. After bumping into the wall beside the entrance, he turned and almost collided with a goblin who beckoned him to follow.

"I pray I don't regret this."

"He's all you've got, so it's not like you have a choice. Use some of that aptitude for magic to show him how it's done," Zarah said as she materialized a parchment to write down notes on the new arrival.

"That is like saying a farmer should show a cook how to prepare meals. While enchanting is a school of magic, it's far removed from summoning a golem or fireball. I've attempted to teach myself some of the basics, but the theorems simply elude me. It's more of an art form than a science."

"The fact remains, the guild sent him instead of a master, so you'll just have to be patient. Speaking of which..."

"Yes? Out with it. I'm not in the mood for games today."

"The artisans wish to meet with you at your earliest convenience."

"Everyone wishes to meet with me at my earliest convenience."

ZHALIX, DRUNDT, AND Yisan sat around the large dining room table in the goblin dining hall. Along with everything else in the room, the table had been recently crafted. The last major attack on the dungeon had scoured many of the rooms clean from anything not made of stone or metal. Fortunately, Drundt's skills, along with the jimps' labor and several carpenters hired from the city, had repaired almost all the damage over the past few weeks, so everything was brand new.

I noticed the artisans' packed bags and belongings stacked against the wall. It seemed the event I had feared had come to pass. "I'd hoped you would stay longer, my friends."

"Aye, I've padded me pockets well while I was here. Haven't made money like this in decades," Drundt said as he nodded toward several enchanted pouches stacked atop one another.

"I believe our callous associate also regrets the fact we will be parting ways immediately, dear King Therion. It has been our pleasure to provide you with our services," Zhalix said with a smile.

"Aye, that too!" Drundt said as he took a huge swig of mead and slammed his tankard on the table. "The dragon woman speaks truly. I've had a grand 'ol time workin' for ya these past few months, but we best be movin' on."

"If you wish to stay longer, I'm sure I could find some work for you," I said. Aside from their invaluable skills, I had to admit I'd miss their company.

"I'm afraid that's quite impossible, dungeon lord," Yisan explained. "We've spent too much time in your dungeon as it is. Even with frequent trips outside, and your Dungeon Heart working to slow the effects, we are slowly becoming attuned to your dungeon. If we spend any more time here, we may never leave. I'm afraid I wish to see more of the world before settling down, and I'm not sure I want to spend my final days buried under tons of rock and dirt."

I smiled. "I understand completely. I knew this day would come soon, but it seems as if you've just arrived here yesterday."

Zhalix took a small sip of wine from a beautiful crystal cup. "We appreciate your business and...the kindness you've shown us. Not all dungeon masters are as forgiving and reasonable as you are."

"Give 'em another two hundred years and he'll be as ornery and hard arsed as the rest of 'em!" Drundt said as he wiped his arm across his mouth.

"That's not necessarily true. Your path is your own. It's unlikely you'll walk a trail of pure evil or one of good. Circumstances disfavor such an outcome, but you've shown considerable restraint and fortitude. Yet at other times you succumbed to the will of Castigous," Yisan said.

"You're speaking of when I...killed the former king?"

Yisan leaned back in his chair and clasped his hands under his chin. "You make it sound so clinical. You killed your father in a fit of rage. In that instant, I saw Castigous' power flow through you. You manipulated the dungeon at a material level.

That shouldn't be possible for your current mastery level from what I can determine. It should be years before you should be able to build constructs or manipulate the environment like that. Either you are a savant, or perhaps the God of Torture Himself has favored you in some way."

"Perhaps both?" Zarah said as she appeared behind me.

"That is also an option," Yisan agreed.

I couldn't explain the sudden rush of power that had come over me in the moment before I cast my father into the Penance of Fate. Whatever it had been, it both thrilled and terrified me. While I had felt a strength and force flow through me unlike anything else I'd ever experienced, the loss of control had been worrisome. It was almost as if I'd stepped back from my physical form and let my darkest desires take control of the situation. Power without control was dangerous.

"Where will you go now that your work here is completed? Will you remain together?" I asked.

Drundt motioned toward a goblin, asking for a refill. "We'll go our separate ways for a bit, takin' a few months off to unwind and shake off the attunement. Can't work in another of Castigous' dungeons until we do, and the gods don't like us around their places of power as long as we got that lingerin' energy in us. They tend to make bad things happen to those that ain't welcome."

Zarah leaned on the back of my chair. "Why can't you work in another dungeon devoted to the God of Punishment and Torture?"

Drundt cast an eye toward Yisan, who brought the legs of his chair back to the ground. "Because the attunement is cumulative. As soon as we entered another dungeon linked to Castigous, the process would pick up again immediately."

"Interesting," I said. Were the dungeons linked in some way? If they all received their powers from a singular god, it made sense if they were somehow connected.

Zhalix stretched and yawned. "I do believe I've had my fill of darkness and the cold, unforgiving stones of this place. While the furnace provides some measure of relief, I yearn to feel the warmth of the sun upon my scales."

"The month of Dead Whisper is almost upon us. As the leaves die and temperatures drop, I'm afraid your desire will be difficult to fulfill," Yisan said.

"Only if I remain in Tharune, my dear," Zhalix said. "Perhaps I will return to the Land of Death. The magma falls are divine at this time of year."

Drundt's eyes lit up. "Aye! While you're there —"

"Perhaps for the right price, I can arrange the transport of some fel powder for you. My prices may have risen slightly, however...I've heard you've come into a windfall of wealth."

"Blast it! Who told ya?" Drundt said as he looked around the table.

"You did — the last time you got drunk with the goblins. It's not like I don't see that you have more bags than we do."

The dark dwarf scratched his beard. "Aye, I might 'ave. I don't remember ya bein' there that night — or any night. Well, don't go tryin' to rip me off just 'cause I got a few gold from this 'lil venture!"

"Indeed. Yet you know you can trust me. What happened to the shipment before last, when you decided to forgo my services?" Zhalix asked.

"Aye, they never did find tha ship. Don't know if it went down in flames, pirates attacked, or some sea monster got 'er. The seas around the Land of Death be swarmin' with all manner of beasties. Lost a lot 'o gold on that business venture."

Drundt and Zhalix leaned closer as they began to discuss business.

"I'll leave you to it, my friends," I said as I stood. The dark dwarf and scalax paused their discussion.

"I'm sorry. It was terrible manners for me to interrupt our farewell discussion for personal business," Zhalix said as she gathered her bags and cases.

"Goblins — assist our visitors with their belongings," I ordered. A dozen goblins entered the room and began gathering the artisans' luggage and tools. These were the goblins that had been incinerated the night the group of masters had attacked. I'd found it had taken much more magic to resurrect them and their belongings than it did for a simple stab wound. Fortunately, Archbishop Phell and Elemental Lord Yolune had contained more than enough magical energy to bring the entire dungeon back to life. A pity it had required their deaths.

On their way out of the door, Drundt stopped and shook my hand. His iron grip met an irresistible counterforce from my sinewy arm. "Lad, you're strong as an ox! Most of yer types are frail and shriveled!"

"Perhaps in a few hundred years," I said as he clapped me on the back and laughed.

"Aye, you've got a long ways ta go," the dwarf said as he led the goblins out. "Maybe we'll work together again someday!" he called over his shoulder. "But ya'd better get some good beer and mead next time!"

Zhalix smiled fondly as she looked down at me. Her razor-sharp teeth belied her gentle and refined demeanor. "Oh, there is no need to be so formal. If I may...?" she asked as she stepped close with her arms open.

"I...don't believe there is any harm in it," I said as I reluctantly opened my arms. She stepped forward and embraced me in a warm hug.

After a moment, she stepped back. "It was a pleasure serving you. I hope my wares met your expectations."

"Your wondrous armor and weapons exceeded my expectations in every way," I replied.

"I'm glad to hear it," she said before her smile turned to a frown. "You *will* be getting them properly enchanted before your next combat? Even your novice enchanter should be able to manage some durability enchantments. I'll be very upset if I return to find all of my work has been dented and chipped to pieces."

"He's told me he is adept at such magic, so I will make sure every piece you crafted is well protected," I promised.

"I'm glad. Please take care, young dungeon lord," she said as she moved past. She paused once more. "And you *will* watch after *them*, won't you? I...let them know I had to go. I'm not sure they understood. I will miss them."

"The arbolisks will be well taken care of. They have the wolves to entertain them if they need company."

"Thank you, Jagen. I hope to return in the future. May your dungeon flourish," Zhalix said as she bowed slightly before turning away.

Yisan stepped forward and smiled. "I wasn't sure about you when we first met. I was convinced you'd meet your end within a week, but you surprised me."

"Aren't you the one that received an arrow to his back?" I asked.

He worked his arm around as if loosening some stiffness. "Yes, and don't think I shall forget that. Why is it the dwarf sacrificed nothing, and he ends up with the lion's share of the payment?"

"I suppose he's a better bargainer than you are," I replied.

Yisan laughed. "That, he is. He's long said I have no business sense and that philosophy and design are not enough to make a living in this world."

I motioned to one of the satchels a goblin carried. "Yet you are leaving here far richer than when you arrived."

"I suppose I do well enough for myself," he said. He grew serious for a moment when next he spoke. "I'm sorry I won't be here to guide or witness what may come next. I believe you're on the verge of advancing to the next level. Your manipulation of the dungeon during the...incident was extraordinary. I wouldn't have expected that from you for at least a few more decades."

I wish I had the elf's knowledge about places of power throughout the realm. Perhaps it would help me learn faster. "Are you sure you won't..."

"I would love to, but it's as the others have said; I can't remain. There will be a withdrawal period as it is. We've lingered here too long. I leave you with one bit of advice, my friend: don't let the power overwhelm you. It's not unlike a flickering flame. It has a myriad of uses, from lighting a candle to cooking a meal. But the flame can also burn down a forest or a city, consuming it all utterly. You must be careful."

"What do you —" I began to ask, but he held up his hand to stop me.

"I've said more than I should already. It's not for me to influence you. You must walk your own path, for good or ill. The gods have plans for us all, my friend."

I grasped his shoulder. "Thank you for your assistance. I hope we meet again someday. Perhaps I'll have the power to create those visions you spoke of."

"Perhaps. I wish you well, King Therion. You bear the weight of two kingdoms on your ample shoulders," the elf said as he moved past me. With a final nod, he beckoned the goblins to follow him out of the dungeon.

CHAPTER THREE
Reconstruction

Publin ran his slender fingers over the stone as if attempting to locate a mechanism or hidden panel. Closing his eyes, he chanted a short spell and focused. "The circuit is fried. Some immense magical force overloaded it. The spell seems to be intact, but I'll have to reconnect the magical link between the stones."

Zarah motioned for him to proceed, but he looked up at me fearfully. "I-I can't do it. The sister stone is miles away. Do you realize how much magic it would take to create that connection? I-I'm just a —"

"Calm yourself. I have magic to spare. Prepare your spell. Open the conduit," I said as I knelt beside the novice enchanter.

"But I don't know how —" he began, but a quick glare silenced him. He placed his hands on the stone and began chanting. After a moment, I felt a slight tug in magic from the stone, as if two magnets sought each other out but were too far apart to bring them together. I let the dungeon's magic flow through me and into the enchanted stone.

A flash of light and a zap knocked Publin on his backside.

"It feels like it's been repaired," Zarah said.

I stood and stepped forward. After the customary disori-
entation of teleportation, I found myself again in the goblin
village. Several children shouted and pointed before running
to greet me. In a moment, dozens of goblins surrounded me.
"Master is back!" "Master has returned!" "Will kinfolk come
back?" they asked anxiously.

"The teleportation stone has been repaired and your fellow
goblins are fine. They will return soon," I said as I motioned for
them to settle down. "All is well."

The looked at each other before cheering in unison. "Celebration!"

The morning sun beat down upon me like a magnifying
glass on a small insect. "I must go, but your clansman will arrive
shortly," I said as I stepped back on the magical stone. Once inside the dungeon, I felt its power flow into me again. It was as
if I were underwater, holding my breath when I was away, and
upon returning I broke the surface and inhaled life-giving air.

"It works. Thank you for your assistance in this matter," I
said to Publin.

"Y-you must have a great deal of magic to so casually jump-
start a connection like that..." he said in awe.

"I do," I said as I turned to Zarah. "Gather the goblins and
let them know the way home has been restored. I believe their
village will be holding a celebration upon their return."

She rolled her eyes. "I'm sure they will. Any reason to drink
is a good reason with this bunch."

"I've noticed. Are you able to continue working, Publin? I
do not know how much effort goes into enchanting."

"I-yes, I can continue. You did the bulk of the effort for that one. A shame I can't use your magic for the other enchantments, but it's a bit different creating an enchantment than reconnecting or recharging one that already existed. You can't assist me on those."

"What of the stone on the felae level? Do you believe it can be repaired?" I asked.

"N-no. There's no connection at all to any paired stone. That link must have been severed a very long time ago. It would have to be created from scratch, I'm afraid. There needs to be at least a residual trace of magic between the two."

"I suspected as much. It was indeed deactivated well over a century ago by the previous lord of this dungeon. Zarah will show you to the next projects I need completed," I said as goblins began to file into the room.

"Home?" "Village?" they asked warily.

"Yes, it's fixed. You may return, resupply, and rejuvenate," I said.

"What about revel and rejoice?" Zarah asked.

"I decided the alliteration would stop at three," I replied as the goblins began lining up to teleport back to their families and friends.

AFTER SOME POSITIVE news regarding the dungeon repairs, I hoped Leath would continue the pattern. He climbed the steps to my throne and knelt. I beckoned for him to rise. To see my former teacher and friend bow before me felt...odd.

"What's the condition of the city this week, old friend?" I asked.

After a deep breath, he gave me the news. "I believe we've lost another ten percent of the population. Mostly the wealthy and their retainers. I'm sorry. We've taken to placing many of them under house arrest, but there are tunnels and secret passages throughout the city, and the guards —"

"Enough. Do you have any good news?"

"Well, it seems the exodus has slowed. I'm not sure we'll lose much more."

"Yes, but at this rate we'll have a city of laborers and poor without any jobs or way to pay them," I said.

"Some are sticking around. They've expressed an interest in meeting with you. It's mostly the smaller guilds and lower castes of nobles."

Leaning back, I thought on the matter. The richest and most powerful had fled, but there were always others looking to take their place. These merchants and nobles saw a vacuum of power and opportunity for new business ventures. The factories, markets, and grand houses of the rich remained. All we needed was someone to fill them. The city would suffer for a period from the loss of wealth, experience, and connections, but we could rebuild it into something perhaps greater than before.

"I'll meet with them. Have Zarah set up the initial meeting. Have you brought someone from the Royal Tax Collection Agency with the records I requested?" I asked.

"I'm afraid many of them abandoned their posts the night the goblins took the castle. A few were killed in the confusion. The only one who remained at his post was a fellow named

Kurth Aderup. Seems he was the second or third in command for the agency. I believe his title was 'Treasurer.' He stuck around for some reason, so he's the best I could find."

"Bring him forth."

A man just outside the entrance to the throne stepped into the throne room. He was balding, with a few strands of hair left and wore thick glasses that exaggerated the size of his eyes. "I'm Treasurer Aderup, Your Highness," he said as he knelt.

"Why did you remain at your post despite the invasion of goblins? Were you frozen with fear or daft?" I asked.

He was caught off guard by my accusation. "N-no, nothing like that. I simply needed to safely hide and store the most important records so they would be safe. It was a lifetime of my work."

"Your work? Are you the only employee of the agency?"

"N-no, I have fellow agents who assist, but I'm the one who creates most of the theorems, charts, formulas, and other methods we use."

"If you are so valuable to the agency and capable, why aren't you the head of it?" I asked.

"I have no interest in that aspect of the work. That would be dealing with the king directly, with daily meetings with the heads of the guilds and houses of nobility."

"So, you are the one who does much of the work while your boss merely entertains the rich clients?"

"I-I'm not sure I would put it that way..." he said.

"It's fine. He's fled the city. In fact, I need someone to replace him. That person is you. Don't worry — I won't force you to entertain the rich and powerful unless you wish to. But

I need someone capable and loyal to assist in running the kingdom. Right now, you are the one I choose."

"Running the kingdom? But I just work with numbers, and create formulas to..."

"The entire world runs on numbers. You've a special gift, and I appreciate talent. Serve me faithfully, and you can have whatever you wish. Gold, magic, women, an estate."

"W-women?" he asked nervously.

I chuckled inwardly. "As I said, whatever you wish. From what I understand, every brothel in the city remains operational despite the exodus of citizens. I need someone to find out which powerful guild leaders and houses of nobility remain in the city. Then I need to find out their financial details, what businesses they are involved in, and their capabilities. Also, if they engaged in any nefarious activities such as slave trade."

"I don't think we keep records of..."

"Thank you for your loyalty, Royal Adviser Aderup. Please locate a capable person to carry out your previous duties at the Royal Tax Collection Agency. I suppose we'll need to train quite a few new workers."

"But I —" he said as a jimp ushered him out of the room.

Leath chuckled. "You're sure he can handle all that? It's a bit much going from crunching numbers to advising the king and hobnobbing with the rich."

"I'm afraid he doesn't have much choice. I'll see that he is well supported. It seems most of my father's advisers and experts fled along with the rest of my family. Which is fortunate for them, because I would have removed them from their posts at the first opportunity. Anyone who supported my father's policies regarding the war, slavery, misleading the people, and his other crimes would need to be removed. There are very few people I trust as much as you, old friend."

"You're the king. I'm just here to serve," Leath said.

"Have you managed to locate my family?" I asked.

"Nothing yet. Of course, with the resources available to them, they could disappear for life if they wished. Your father had a lot of contacts throughout the country, so it will take time to visit them all."

"Continue the search and keep me updated on what you find."

"It shall be done," Leath said. I expected him to leave, but he stood silently, as if contemplating.

"You have something you wish to ask?" I asked.

"I...was just wondering what your endgame is here, Jag - I mean, my lord. Are you going to remain confined to this dungeon while also ruling over the kingdom? As you heard from Lord Yolune, we may be able to cure you of your link to this place. You could return to the surface and live a normal life. If only the people could see their new king, it would help quell the fears and uncertainty that run rampant. My name carries a lot of weight, but the people want a proper ruler."

"The people now have a ruler who cares about their lives and welfare. It's simply a matter of making them realize that," I replied. "They will have greater freedom and a truthful flow of information instead of fear mongering and lies from their leaders."

Leath shook his head. "That's the thing you don't understand, son. Many of them don't want to know the truth. They don't want that kind of responsibility or freedom. They want someone to tell them they'll be safe."

"We will have to put that to the test, old friend. I don't believe they've ever experienced the things you claim they don't want."

"I suppose you know best. I tend to keep out of these matters, and you've probably learned more from your books and studies than I ever will," Leath said as he ran his hand through his hair. "Just keep in mind — experience is the best teacher. I've always said history books were written to protect the present."

"Let's just hope I can maintain control over the kingdom until I gain that experience," I replied.

"If you can't, there won't be much of a city to rule over," Leath replied.

CHAPTER FOUR
Haunted Dreams

The cool night breeze rushed through the open windows as the sheer drapes flapped to and fro in an almost violent manner. The hairs on my neck stood on end as the air flowed over my exposed body. Yet, another's body behind me generated all the warmth I needed. I turned my head upward to see Aiyla's bemused face looking down upon me.

"You find my lap to be a comfortable pillow, I take it?" she asked as she caressed my hair.

I smiled. "I wish to never leave it. For any reason."

"I believe we both have responsibilities that would preclude that," she said as she doused a candle with a golden, ornate snuffer that elongated to reach several feet away. Once the flame had been doused, the magical tool retracted automatically. The right side of her face was now ensconced in shadow.

"Responsibilities be damned. Our only responsibilities are those to each other," I said. "We are both pawns of our kingdoms."

"Yes, but your people do not die as mine do. I cannot allow that, Love," she said as she turned on the massive bed of silky pillows and snuffed another candle.

I ran my hand along her supple leg. "You are right. I won't allow it either. Together, we will bring peace to both of our kingdoms. Then we will live the rest of our days in utter contentment."

Now her entire face was hidden in shadow. She traced a finger across my features, at last coming to rest on my lips. "I am content now. I wish we could run away and leave this all behind, but that is not what fate has in store for us, my love."

"This is taking too long," I said as I cast a spell that doused the rest of the candles. She giggled as she slipped my head out from under her lap and nimbly flipped around to lie beside me in the bed.

"You're too impatient. The act of seduction is an art form. It makes the final embrace that much more pleasurable."

"Is that what your people believe?" I asked.

"Indeed. I had planned for another hour of temptation and teasing."

"That sounds more like torture than pleasure. Simply seeing you is more temptation than I can endure," I said as I slipped my hand behind her head. She leaned in, her lips brushing mine in the darkness.

"Then you are in for a very torturous night, my love," she whispered as she pulled me close.

Her warm lips locked with mine, the fires of passion burning hotter than her desert sun. Then...the room became cold. The breeze from the window turned into a frozen, howling wind. The thin blankets on the bed no longer provided comfort. I clung to Aiyla, attempting to keep the both of us warm with our love. Despite my efforts, she turned cold and hard, like a corpse.

A beam of moonlight filtered through the window, illuminating her face. I gasped as her rotted skull looked back at me, twisted with hatred. "How could you let this happen to me, Jagen? I loved you!" she shrieked before her bony, clawed fingers reached out for me. I screamed and thrust her away.

I willed for light to banish the darkness. Slowly, the magical orbs sprang to life. I was back in my bedroom in the dungeon. It took me a long moment to gather my bearings. With astonishment, I realized someone was in the bed with me.

"Helatha! What are you doing here?" I demanded. The soul snatcher was entangled in the blankets. Her bare skin peeked out from underneath the covers.

She flipped her hair from her face. "I...thought you could use some company. You've seemed overwhelmed with your mantles of leadership, so I came to help you...find release."

"You...decided this?"

"Every leader should have a partner to help them shoulder the burdens they take upon themselves. You've been too preoccupied to notice, but I'm willing to help you. I can be your queen, your dungeon mistress."

She reached out and put her hand to the side of my face as she let the blanket fall away. Closer she came, until her face was mere inches from mine. "Let me help you, Master." She moved in and kissed me again. Her cold lips offered nothing of love, only lust.

I pushed her away. "You presume too much. It was you who intruded in my dream — my dream of Aiyla. You came into my thoughts and slipped into her form, replacing her. You invaded my privacy."

"But I merely wanted to...you don't find this body attractive?"

I glanced over the stolen cleric's body but grew angrier at Helatha's attempt to seduce me as I slept. "You are starved for love and attention yourself, so you decided I would be the one to fulfill your needs."

She was quiet for a moment before answering. "It has been so long trapped here. No one but corpses and swine and insects. I just need a little..."

"I'm not your toy, soul snatcher. I do not need your deathly entertainments. How dare you presume to take what you need from me? Who are you to invade my dreams and replace Aiyla with yourself?" I said as I rose and clothed myself in a robe. The volume of my voice grew as I thought more on her deception and violation of my sacred dreams.

"You're my minion, nothing more. If you are feeling lonely and require the need for companionship, see Ho'Scar. Take your pick from his prisoners."

"It's...not the same. You're..."

"I'm your master. I do not need you to fulfill my desires. Could you see my love for Aiyla when you invaded my mind against my will? Could you feel the bond we shared?"

She turned away. "I...could. I've never felt anything like it. I wish...I wish I could."

"You can't take her place. No one can. Do not violate my trust again, or I'll have Ho'Scar punish you."

"I just wanted...If you must love a dead woman, then why not me?"

"My love for Aiyla is inviolate and forever. Leave, Helatha. Do not invade my mind again — for both of our sakes."

She looked at me for a moment, as if hoping I'd change my mind. When I did not, she slowly slid out of bed and gathered her clothes before leaving.

"That was a bit harsh, don't you think?" Zarah asked.

"Harsh would be placing her in the torture chamber for a week or disposing of her. My emotions are not to be toyed with. The memories of Aiyla are sacred. None may meddle with my one source of pure happiness."

"You'll have to move on, eventually. You're going to live a very long life if you remain the dungeon's lord and master. You wish to live in loneliness and pain for all of those years? You need to let Aiyla go. She's not coming back, but you're here, now."

"I'll never let her go. No one will ever replace her. I won't settle for substandard affection when I know what we had together."

"Surely something is better than nothing?"

"Perhaps for most people — not for me."

"You may change your tune in a hundred years — perhaps even two years. You're still relatively new to this, unlike Helatha and myself. Aiyla is fresh in your mind, but she will fade."

"I'll never change my mind concerning Aiyla...and obviously you had a hand in this scheme."

"What makes you say that?"

"Helatha only has access to the door on her level. You would have had to open the doors for her as she came down."

"I guess I'm not quite as sneaky as I thought. I just thought...you could use a break from your responsibilities.

Now, the whole thing was her idea — don't get me wrong. But I did agree to it."

"I...appreciate the thought, but this is not an area I wish for you or her to interfere in. Please do not do it again, Zarah." The Dungeon Heart probably thought she was slaying two hydra heads with one flaming stroke by fulfilling Helatha's desires and providing me with companionship, but it simply made me feel the loss of Aiyla anew.

"I'm sorry —"

"Just...don't." I said as I climbed back into bed.

I willed the dream with Aiyla to return as I succumbed to my weariness, but the rest of the night was filled with nothing but empty darkness.

CHAPTER FIVE
The New Blood

I wasn't sure why or when the goblin dining hall had become the dungeon's normal meeting place, but it had. Logistically, it made sense; it was large enough to house over a hundred people, and its large table could seat several dozen. The fireplace radiated a hospitable warmth that seemed to set people at ease. Personally, it was reassuring that a small army of goblins was at my beck and call should something go amiss. I was sure it was somewhat intimidating for guests to see the armed patrols pass by the door regularly — which could work in my favor during negotiations. Of course, the goblins' penchant for drunken debauchery led to more than a few last-minute cleaning sessions before important guests arrived.

"All rise for King Jagen Therion," Kurth stated with authority. It seemed his new position had given the ex-treasurer a bit more confidence. I hoped his internal fortitude could match his exterior demeanor.

The five people seated stood until I had seated myself at the head of the table.

"Allow me to introduce those gathered before you, my lord," Kurth said. I nodded in agreement.

"Seated to your left is the head of House Keluthe, Lady Keluthe. Her family controls the second largest shipping company in Tharune. They have contacts in every major country across Derode."

Lady Keluthe held a remarkable air of elegance about her. The matriarch of House Keluthe looked to be in her low sixties. Thin, tall, and with pale blue eyes, she nodded as Kurth introduced her. She wore an elegant glimmering gold and red layered dress with a veiled hat and layers of jewelry consisting of dozens of yellow gold bangles and exotic necklaces gathered from around the world. It appeared she kept much of the finer trade merchandise for herself. "It's a pleasure to meet the new king at last," she said in a stern voice.

"Likewise, Lady Keluthe," I said.

"To her left sits Chuph Nevorn. He's taken it upon himself to head up the labor guild after the rather sudden...disappearance of the last guild master," Kurth stated.

Chuph was a young, well-muscled youth with tousled red hair and angry freckles. He looked almost as if he was spoiling for a fight, even at this very moment. "Aye, we've heard you're different from your father, and I came to see if them rumors were true. We managed to drive off the old leadership and now we want things to change for the workers in New Vadis. We want better pay and guarantees for our safety and work conditions."

I smiled. "Then our desires align. I'm here to see there is a new way going forward. One that shares the wealth between the workers and their employers."

Chuph gave me a suspicious stare before nodding in agreement. If he truly had the support of the city's laborers, and their best interests at heart, he could be just the man I was looking for.

Kurth continued with the introductions. "To your right sits Lorena Sharde. She's assumed control of the merchant's guild at my request."

I was surprised Kurth had made such a decision without my input, but after a moment, I decided I was grateful someone was willing to make decisions without my authority. Lorena's long, blonde hair reached down past her shoulders and she looked fit enough to have served in the Royal Guard. Her calm, cold stare gave the impression she was used to her orders being obeyed.

"I hope we can work together on many of the issues that have sprung up since many of the leaders of the city have fled or have been imprisoned at your command," she said without a hint of fear.

I smiled. "That's why we are here, Lorena. I was perhaps a bit...overzealous in my decisions after assuming leadership. I'm a reasonable man and willing to negotiate — within certain boundaries."

"Thank you for your consideration, Your Highness." She began writing in one of several notebooks she'd brought along.

"To her right is Lord Fedege, head of House Fedege, one of the oldest houses in New Vadis. Lord Fedege deals in more...illicit activities within the city," Kurth said as diplomatically as he could.

Lord Fedege's curly black hair and moustache were almost comical in their appearance. Was he attempting to look like the blackguards he controlled? He was like a fairytale villain come to life. Adorned all in black, he wore leathers that an adventurer might have worn. The empty sheath at his side indicated he could at least defend himself in combat. "I wasn't aware the king was so handsome," he said.

Kurth stammered a reply. "You presume much, Lord Fedege. Do not speak to King Therion in such a familiar manner."

"I...apologize. I perhaps allow my emotions and thoughts to overwhelm me. If you wish to know of the dealings in the underworld, it would be my pleasure to show them to you, Your Highness," Lord Fedege said.

"I can appreciate honesty, Lord Fedege. I know there have been certain activities that were legal under my father — such as the sale and trade of slaves. I'm sure you are aware I've decreed this practice is barbaric and will no longer be tolerated. While I am willing to overlook certain criminal activities, there are some I will not compromise on. Is that understood?" I asked.

"Yes, completely, Your Highness. My family has dwelt within the borders of your family's kingdom for generations. As the laws change, so change our ways. We simply operate on the...fringe of society. As you may know, being against the law and against the wishes of the kingdom were two different matters under your late father's rule," Lord Fedege explained.

"I...am aware of the hypocrisy of my father. However, we will not have two sets of laws under my leadership. What applies to the citizenry will apply to the nobles. All are equal in the eyes of the law."

"I...see," Lord Fedege said. "What a refreshing viewpoint."

I was unable to tell if he was mocking me or genuinely intrigued by my ideals.

Kurth began to introduce the last member of our meeting but was interrupted. "Now I would like to introduce —"

"Carine Mordu, Your Highness! Head of the newly formed 'Taste of Adventure' adventurers' guild, at your service. When the rest of the questing guilds up and left, I figured there needed to be *someone* who would organize anyone who wanted to explore the world, gain fame and fortune and destroy evil monsters — err, no offense, Your Highness. I know you're master of this dungeon full of creepy monsters as well as our king, so it might seem like our philosophies will bump heads, but as my dear grandpappy used to say..." the stout young female gnome gushed. She had brown hair put up into a bun, large glasses, green eyes, and was apparently very...energetic. She continued to ramble on about her new guild and their mission statement for another five minutes. I wasn't sure if she ever paused to breathe.

I needed to move the meeting forward or else the others and myself would lose interest. "Thank you for your...enthusiasm, Carine, but we must press on. Present to me the problems you face currently and vision for the future of our great city. Let's start with Lady Keluthe," I said. I had no way of knowing which of these people I could trust, which were competent, or which would be at each other's throats upon immediately leaving, so I would need to set up a series of questions to determine the stronger leaders.

"Thank you, King Therion. I've prepared a short list of the most pressing issues within the city. I've provided a copy for you," Lady Keluthe said as she passed a scroll down the table. Her short list was almost a page long.

"I also have a list," Lorena said as she set a large bag upon the table and began to look through it.

"Please read mine after hers," Chuph said as he leaned forward to pass his down.

"Do you have a parchment...and a quill?" Carine said as she watched the other more-prepared leaders rifle through their belongings.

The meeting continued for two hours. As predicted, they each had suspicions and grievances with each other and the previous leaders. I instructed them that any leaders who fled the city to protect their wealth would be stripped of their titles and authority would be passed on to those who stayed, swore allegiance to me, and proved their worth.

The group had a great deal of experience between the lot of them. Many of them had served beside or under the previous leaders, so they were well versed in running business operations. I just needed to determine if they had stayed to advance their own interests or if there was some other reason. I would need a competent council if I were going to hold the city together, especially since I did not have the luxury of presenting myself in person to the citizenry.

However, after several hours of serving as an intermediary between competing interests and factions, it was becoming apparent that my patience had limits. These newcomers spent the entire time testing me and prodding for weaknesses in myself and their competitors. I lacked experience and the wisdom of age in their eyes. Yet I held the advantage of position and willpower.

"Thank you for your time. Zarah and the guards will see you out," I abruptly announced in the middle of a speech Chuph had apparently prepared in advance.

"But...Your Highness, the meeting has only been in session for a few hours. It's customary for these gatherings to last at least two to three times longer," Lady Keluthe said as if she were admonishing a child.

I stood. "I'm not one for customs. In fact, I prefer to toss the old ways out of a very high window. I have other matters to attend to, but I believe we've laid the base for a new framework of governance in the city. As you know, many citizens are afraid. Some of them chose to flee with the old aristocracy. Those who stayed need to feel safe and secure. There are those attempting to spread rumors and discord throughout the city. I want you to assist me in stopping this. We must keep the exodus from continuing. I want you to raise wages for your workers. I want you to provide them with benefits and bonuses for staying. Assist them in finding housing and any other issues they may have."

"But, Your Highness, our funds are depleted from the —" Lord Fedege began to say before I held up a hand to silence him.

"You'll be compensated by the Royal Treasury. Make arrangements with Kurth for your intermediate operating expenses," I said as I nodded toward my new Royal Adviser.

"It will be as you say, Your Highness," Kurth stated as he pulled out a parchment.

"Pardon me, King Therion, but I fail to see what you gain from funding us with the kingdom's coffers," Lady Keluthe said as the others stood to leave.

"Think of it as...a stabilizing investment for the kingdom. We will make it worthwhile for our remaining citizens and leaders to stay. Eventually, this should be returned in tax revenue once the city calms itself and begins to operate normally."

"And what's to stop us from just takin' yer money and doin' what we see fit with it? Skimming some off the top for ourselves?" Chuph asked suspiciously.

"You'd be exchanging temporary immediate financial gain over long-term financial benefit. Imagine if the labor guild swelled to three times its size, and the workers were well funded. Would a few thousand gold be worth the loss of decades of growth? There's also the fact I'd use you to test my newest torture devices in the dungeon if I found out."

Chuph massaged the back of his head in apparent discomfort. "Aye, ya perhaps have a good point, Your Highness."

"Why would you even think to steal from the king? He's here to help us get on our feet, and you want to abuse his friendship and undo all the hard work he's put into helping the kingdom over the past few weeks? You should be ashamed to even think such thoughts, you...you...ruffian!" Carine said as she stood on her chair and leaned on the table to get closer to Chuph's height.

"I...appreciate your loyalty, Miss Mordu, but please calm yourself," I said. The gnome was indeed feisty. "We must all work together to achieve what is best for the city."

Carine hopped down from her chair and nodded. "Damn straight we do. I mean...I agree, Your Highness."

"We'll meet again in a week in order to discuss progress. Be careful — there are forces working against us who wish to resume their control," I said as I rose to see the leaders to the door.

The new city leaders and Kurth filed out.

"What do you think?" Zarah asked as she materialized on the table with her legs dangling over the sides.

"Perhaps this will work. They seem fairly intelligent and capable. It's not as if we have a lot of options."

"Do you trust them?"

"Of course not. Despite Kurth's recommendations, I know virtually nothing of these people. We will have to keep tabs on them to see who we can trust. Are your bugs in place?"

"As you spoke to them, several roaches made their way into their bags. We'll have at least some eyes on their affairs despite our distance from the city. I couldn't help but notice that so far, we've had no leadership from the Uxper Orthodoxy present. Did they refuse your invitation?"

I couldn't help but smile. "They state they cannot meet with a representative who serves the false god, Castigous. They consider it blasphemy to even meet with me, especially after I've captured and tortured some of their leaders."

"That does tend to put a damper on friendly relationships," Zarah admitted.

"Indeed. Yet I do not want to be on friendly terms with them. I consider their worship of money and their hidden sins to be unconscionable. I'm considering banning them from the city."

"Don't most of the citizens follow Uxper? What's taking their religion going to do to their morale?"

"A god who puts wealth above all else shouldn't provide morale to anyone. He's a cruel, selfish god if he exists."

"His clerics and priests get their power from somewhere. It seems to me he must exist," Zarah said as she held out the palm of her hand and caused a small roach to materialize in it.

If the god of wealth, profit, and success existed and his followers were actually doing his bidding, perhaps he should be the one punished in a torture chamber. I wondered if such a thing were possible. Zarah dropped the roach from one hand to the other in a series of motions that left the insect disoriented. "Still tormenting Duke Merromont?"

Zarah brought the insect closer to her ear and listened. "I have so few hobbies other than my music. What good is a dungeon if we can't torture the truly guilty?"

"Does he ever say anything useful?"

"Not particularly. Cursing and begging, mostly. He says he can help you rule if you return him to human form."

"I have no way to do that, and I'm fairly certain he was dead or almost dead when we tossed him into the Penance of Fate. Returning him to his human form may result in his final death."

"Do you hear that, Duke of Scum? The Master says you shall remain a roach forever. Think of my mother and brother as you scurry amongst the cracks in the walls," Zarah said as she set the roach on the ground and sent him away.

I sat and leaned back in the chair. The embers of the fire glowed dimly in the massive fireplace. Two of the torches had died down over the course of the meeting. A goblin noticed my gaze and began to swap them out, but I motioned him away. The atmosphere in the room felt cozy at the moment.

I realized that I was content — as if perhaps this was going to work out after all. With Leath and Kurth coordinating with the new city leaders, it would relieve my shoulders of some of the burden.

"Draw me a pint of mead," I said to a nearby goblin guard. He looked confused for a moment before doing as ordered. "Make sure it's a clean mug," I shouted after him.

"A celebratory drink? How unlike you," Zarah said as she sat in the chair to my right. Due to her incorporeal form, I'd be drinking alone.

A strange construct materialized in the air before us. A mass of glowing blue connected crystals floated in the air in concentric circles. The device resembled an unbelievably large snowflake.

Zarah looked at the surprise on my face before explaining, "Another instrument I dreamed up. What do you think?"

The blue glow of the crystals illuminated her face in the darkened chamber. She smiled demurely then closed her mouth as if she were embarrassed by her fangs.

"Beautiful," I whispered.

She traced her fingers across the floating gems, causing each to turn golden as her delicate fingers brushed them. They hummed as she did so. Soon, she wove a beautiful melody, her hands flitting about as if working some magical loom. The dazzling lights were as much entertainment as the music. It was mesmerizing and relaxing. The goblin attendant set a pint in front of me, and I drew a long sip. It was surprisingly good. As Zarah's song continued, I felt slightly lightheaded and slumped down in my chair.

When her song had finished, I said, "Marvelous. I've never heard anything like it. Your ability to create not just music but new instruments is a testament to your genius. What will you call this one?"

Despite her red-tinted skin, I believe she blushed a bit. "I was thinking of calling it the Crystal Cascade. What do you think?"

"Excellent. I enjoy every time you play anything for me." Yawning, I noticed the fire had almost gone out completely. It must have been very late. "I believe I'll rest very well tonight. For the first time in ages, I feel like this may all come together."

CHAPTER SIX
Unknown

The voice, hollow and deep, reverberated through my mind. At first a whisper, I strained to hear the words. I felt as if I should turn my head or move to locate the source of the voice, but I had no body. It was as if I were the darkness itself. Immobile and still, simply a vessel to contain the world.

Yet, the voice slowly increased in volume, as if the source were coming to me. "They're coming," it whispered. "They're coming," it said again, louder.

I attempted to speak, but I did not have that ability. I merely thought, "Who? Who is coming?"

"They're here!" the voice boomed, shattering my thoughts and my being. The darkness cracked as light poured into the scene. My eyes now opened wide, I realized I was in my bed. It had merely been a nightmare. I breathed a sigh of relief and relaxed as I looked around for some clothing. My gaze fell upon Orgun's staff, which sat propped up against the wall.

While I could sense the power within the relic, I'd been unable to tap into it. At times, it felt...alive. I would perhaps need more magical stamina and experience in the mystic arts before being able to wield such a powerful artifact.

After locating my pants and slipping them on, I was startled to find Zarah had materialized directly beside me. "We may have a problem."

"We always have a problem. In fact, we have nothing but problems," I said as I slipped on a shirt.

"No, I mean...something serious. The guards at the dungeon entrance are gone."

"What do you mean 'gone'? There are ten Royal Guard stationed there. Show me."

She pulled up an image of the entrance. It was still early morning and dark outside. The sun wouldn't rise for another hour or two. Indeed, no one was present. Their lanterns and torches were gone, along with any other belongings such as chairs or barricades. It was as if they'd packed up completely and left their posts.

"Treason," I growled. Someone had paid them to abandon their posts just as much of my army had been bought off over the past few months.

"Wait...look there," Zarah said as she moved the vision closer. On the ground just outside, a small object rested in the dirt. It took a moment of focusing to realize what it was.

"A finger," I whispered. The bloody digit looked as if it had just been severed moments ago. Yet there was no evidence of a battle or bodies. "Show me the jail area."

Zarah did as instructed, carefully moving throughout the cells. The skeletons remained positioned at their posts undisturbed. Each cell remained locked. All looked to be in order. It seemed we had gotten lucky and the main attack hadn't started yet. They'd taken out our human guards, but hadn't entered the dungeon.

"Wait...something's wrong," Zarah said as she moved the vision out of the jail and down the hall. It soon came upon the open door to the next level.

"Did you open that?" I asked.

She shook her head, a look of confusion on her face. "No. The dungeon is sealed completely."

"Show me the skeleton who holds the key."

The image zoomed back to the jail and focused on one cell. A skeleton stood inside, holding its hand out through the bars. An empty hand.

"What's happening?" I asked.

"They...it's as if they've gone into a state of rest again. Someone's turned them off," Zarah said as she closed her eyes and focused. The inanimate skeletons shook their heads as if awakening from slumber.

"Where's Ho'Scar?" I asked.

She moved her vision down to the dungeon and searched for the torturer.

The large pig-man labored over a prisoner, sewing up a tear in the flesh of the woman's arm. "Can't 'ave ya gettin' infected and dyin' on me, can we, beautiful?" Ho'Scar said as he focused on gently moving the needle through the skin and back again. His large, meaty hoof-hands were ill-suited to the task, but he was soon finished.

"There we go, now to just — what? Who are you?" he said as he turned around. The image went dark.

"What happened? Bring it back!"

Zarah looked confused as she focused. "I-I can't. Something's blocking me. The entire level is lost to me. I can feel something is there, but I can't see it."

"Armor," I said to the nearest jimp. It scuttled off to retrieve my now-enchanted armor and sword. Publin's best efforts had resulted in a level three durability enchantment on the armor and a level two durability and level one honing enchantment on Purgatory. It would be enough to prevent damage against moderately enchanted weapons.

"Alert each level that we have intruders," I said as I began to don the armor. "Notify Publin he should seek shelter in one of the hidden portal rooms or in the throne room." Zarah stood unmoving.

"Zarah! What's come over you? Do as I say!"

She jumped as if she'd been lost in her thoughts. "I-I haven't seen this...it's been so long, but..."

"Calm yourself. What are you trying to say?"

"This-this is like the other time. This happened before. With Orgun...it was the end. I-I thought I was going to die..."

She was going into shock. Was the mysterious force attacking the dungeon somehow affecting her mind? She would be of no use to me if she continued to sink into madness. I couldn't grab hold of her to bring her back to reality. Yet, as the Dungeon's Master, there were other ways to affect its occupants.

"ZARAH," I boomed mentally, sending forth a wave of my willpower to shock her back to reality.

She staggered and almost fell, but she came to her senses. "I'm...sorry."

"What do you mean this has happened before?" I asked as I resumed donning my armor.

"This is like the incident that shut down the dungeon the first time. T-the group came in and went through our defenses like they weren't even there. Either rendering them useless or destroying them. It's like we were powerless to stop them. I couldn't get in touch with Orgun because he was off in his sanctum and by the time he realized something was wrong, it was too late."

"How did the dungeon survive? What happened?"

"I-I don't remember the end. I remember them making it into the Dire Hall...then the throne room, then nothing. They did something to me, I think. Weeks later, Orgun brought me back from the darkness, but the dungeon's magic was almost gone, and many of the creatures had been wiped out."

"How are they overcoming our defenses and blocking your sight?"

"I wish I knew. The first time, so long ago...that party...it was just me, and I couldn't stop them...I hadn't been that scared since Duke Merromont..."

I hadn't seen Zarah so unsure of herself before. Whatever had happened those many decades ago must have shaken her to her core. "This time you are not alone. We will defeat these invaders and wring their secrets from them," I said as I lowered my helm.

"Bring me Xagrim and Toxin. If this group manages to make it to this level, we'll meet them in the Dire Hall."

"Wait...I can see the torture chamber again," Zarah said as she pulled the image up before us. Other than Ho'Scar lying unmoving on the ground, the room looked undisturbed.

"They left his key ring, though," Zarah said as she zoomed in on the torturer's body.

"No, look closer. The key to the next level has been removed," I said as I studied Ho'Scar. There wasn't a visible mark on his body, but he was deceased. Nothing in the room had been disturbed. He hadn't even drawn his weapon. It appeared as if he had put up no fight at all.

Xagrim and Toxin awaited us in the throne room.

"Intruders?" Xagrim asked.

"This is like the group that almost destroyed us, Xagrim. This is not a normal party," Zarah said with a slight tremble in her voice.

Xagrim blinked several times. I don't think I'd ever seen the death knight do that before. "Like...before?"

"Silence. I do not care what happened one and a half centuries ago. We will defeat this new group and find out how they are subverting the dungeon's defenses and minions," I ordered. "They've defeated Ho'Scar with little effort, so we must be wary. We don't know how many there are or their capabilities. Can you see the goblin level?"

"I can see only bits and pieces. Here..." Zarah said as she focused. A fuzzy image of one of the halls revealed a dispatched party of goblins. Again, it seemed they'd not put up much of a fight. The hunter's quiver was still filled with arrows and the warriors' weapons had not been drawn.

"How are they getting by our defenses without any resistance? Is it some form of invisibility? What do you think, Toxin?"

The ex-leader of Inevitable Oblivion stared intently at the scene. "No, I do not believe it is a stealth tactic. The way the bodies are arranged indicates they were attacked from the front, not rear. Yet they did not fight. They saw their attackers yet had no chance."

Zarah attempted to move throughout the level but ran into the mysterious interference periodically. Each scene revealed the invaders were easily moving through the level.

"What of the goblins in the barracks?" I asked. The lot of them were most likely hung over and drunk from the previous night, but as long as they were not on active duty, I usually did not care.

"They haven't been disturbed. It's as if the intruders know exactly where the key is on each level. They avoid unnecessary distractions and focus on obtaining the key. This is exactly what happened before," Zarah said. "They've opened the door to the church level, but they haven't exited yet."

"This is maddening. I feel as if we should rush to meet them so that we can join forces with either Helatha or the arbolisks, but we could fall prey to this mysterious force and leave the throne room unprotected," I said as Zarah's image of the goblin level cleared. "Have the wolves returned from their hunt?"

"No. The young arbolisks are alone," Zarah said.

Blast. I would have had more faith in the inexperienced arbolisks if they were joined with the two crimson wolves. We allowed the wolves the freedom to leave the dungeon periodically so that they wouldn't become attuned to it permanently. While they had become creatures of the dungeon, they were similar to the goblins in that they were not bound to it.

"Keep monitoring the situation. I'm going to check the traps in the Dire Hall to make sure they are primed and functioning," I said as I left the room. Without a regular influx of adventurers, we'd grown lax in security. The Royal Guard at the entrance acted as a deterrent to any potential adventurers, but they seemed redundant, as no one had sought to attack the dungeon since I'd officially made it known the King of Tharune served as the dungeon's master.

The Dire Hall was so large, it took twenty minutes to inspect each trap. While it was unlikely an adventurer would stumble upon one, the true purpose of the traps was to act as additional firepower we could use against enemies by pushing or leading them into harm's way.

I returned to the throne room. "Any word on Helatha's level?"

Zarah shook her head. "I can only say the door leading to the arbolisk level hasn't been opened yet. I believe the group hasn't defeated Helatha."

"Perhaps she's destroyed them. She proved to be a strong counter to Leath's party of master adventurers," I said.

"I hope you're right."

An hour passed, then two. Zarah's attempts to peer into the church level proved futile. The anticipation of attack grew unbearable.

"Perhaps you could go up and fight alongside the arbolisks, as you said?" Zarah suggested.

"The younglings are immune to each other's breath attacks, but they do not have much combat experience. It would be too risky for us to be around them. Even if we have the antidote, becoming rooted for even a split second in battle could prove disastrous."

"Are you sure you can revive them if they are destroyed?" Zarah asked.

"We will have to find out, eventually. I believe as long as they are not disintegrated or otherwise completely destroyed, it should prove possible. Otherwise, we may not have enough magic." I cast a glance at the Soul Sphere. The glowing orb appeared to be perhaps eighty percent full. It should be enough to resurrect the entire dungeon if needed.

"Perhaps you should get some rest. The group may be camping for the day in order to replenish themselves," Zarah suggested.

"No. I'll remain awake in order to monitor the situation. I do not want to be groggy if they should somehow slip to this level. Having a rogue slit my throat as I doze would be an ignoble end."

Several hours later, Zarah gasped. "Helatha is dead."

"Show me."

The interior of the church was filled with ghouls, but instead of a battle, it looked as if they had attended a sermon. They sat in the pews facing forward, immobile and silent. Nothing was out of order or disturbed.

"Where is Helatha?" I asked.

The vision swerved and panned up to the ceiling, where a ghastly vision awaited. Helatha's body was nailed to the wooden beams that held up the ceiling.

"By the gods..." Zarah whispered.

"She's been posed to send a message to us. It looks familiar..." I said. Her legs were crossed one over the other and her hands were folded in front of her chest. Barbed wire had been wrapped around her body. "It's...the symbol of Castigous."

"But...why go through the trouble?" Zarah asked. "What does it mean?"

"They want us on edge and fearful. Do not let them intimidate you. Have they exited to the arbolisk level?" I asked. Although my words were meant to inspire, I had to admit I was more than a little concerned. While Leath's party had been able to overcome our minions and traps, it had left evidence of massive battles. Each level today had been conquered with childish ease. This was no ordinary party of adventurers we faced.

Zarah displayed the exit from the arbolisk level. The landing room's door remained closed. "They haven't — wait, it's opening."

The door slowly swung open, revealing the pitch-black landing room. Did the enemy not need light to see? Had they doused the torches before opening the door?

A single glowing eye opened from the darkness before Zarah's vision was dispelled like before.

"I will destroy these interlopers," Xagrim said as he smashed his hand into the palm of his other. "I will not fail again."

It almost sounded as if the death knight was trying to convince himself. I wondered what had transpired when the dungeon almost fell all those years ago.

"Maybe you should hold back and let Toxin and Xagrim face them until we see what they are," Zarah suggested.

"We may not have the luxury of analyzing them once they are here. A full-frontal assault will be our best option," I said.

Another hour passed before Zarah interrupted the silence. "I think they're now in the forest."

"Can you present an image?"

"I'm trying, but...it's not working," Zarah said with frustration.

"Instead of attempting to focus on the group directly, pull as far back as possible. Try an overhead view of the forest from the top of the cavern ceiling. Perhaps there is a range to their ability to shroud themselves," I said.

A blacked-out image appeared before us, but in a moment, a faded view of the top of the trees appeared. As it pulled back, the picture solidified until we could see the forest below. The view continued to retreat and improve in quality until we were looking down from the massive ceiling of the forest. Unfortunately, from this distance, it would be difficult to determine what was going on below.

"There they are," Zarah said as a trio of figures emerged from a side cave onto the rim of the forest. The figures wore black and red cloaks that covered them completely. They moved slowly and methodically, as if they were religious pilgrims making a yearly journey to pay respects to a holy place.

"Three? A mere three people have dispatched all of our defenses?" I said.

The small group made their way to the ramp that led down into the forest. Due to the distance of Zarah's vision, it was hard to follow their path through the trees and foliage.

"Look, the arbolisks!" Zarah said as the vision panned over to the arbolisk den that housed the doorway down. The three young drakes seemed agitated, as if ready for combat.

"Perhaps they've caught the scents of the intruders," Toxin said.

The group emerged from the trees. At the distance we were viewing the action, it was almost impossible to determine the details of the fight. We could simply see the arbolisks charging as the group moved about.

"Look at the flashes of green. They're unleashing their breath attacks," I said. One of the small figures stopped moving for a moment. "I believe he's rooted." Before the arbolisks could move in, a flash of crimson light flared like a small star erupting. The three lizards fled away from the intruders, almost running into walls, trees, or any obstacles that crossed their paths.

"Some type of fear spell?" Zarah asked.

"Perhaps. If it is, it should wear off in approximately thirty to sixty seconds. The arbolisks' plant-based physiology makes them somewhat resistant to mental attacks that were designed for regular fauna." I began counting down in my mind as the fleeing minions found their way to the ramp and scampered up it. Moments later, they had disappeared into the labyrinthine tunnels that made up the rest of the level.

"Five minutes. That was no fear spell that I know of. Look, the other two intruders have returned to their companion," I said. Moments later, the three of them slowly moved to the lake. They had healed or dispelled their companion that may have been affected by the transformative breath attacks of the arbolisks. The trio appeared utterly confident the creatures would not return as they focused on the lake. It was like they knew exactly where every key on each level was hidden and how to overcome the minions or traps.

It was impossible to see their exact actions, but moments later, they made their way to the door down and exited the level.

"They didn't even have to search the lake!" Zarah exclaimed.

She was right. These invaders seemed to know every inch of our dungeon. Had they been informed about the layout and traps from visitors? Had I been too confident in allowing people to venture into the dungeon? With the might of the Royal Guard and military behind me, along with our reputation for defeating a high-level party of adventurers, I had assumed no one would dare attack us. Yet here was a party easily defeating each of our defenses without trouble.

"Come. The next level will present little challenge. We must await their arrival in the Dire Hall," I said.

The massive death knight and undead rogue joined me as I took up position in the giant empty room of gleaming black stone.

"What about your combination wall?" Zarah asked as she joined us. She wore her combat outfit, although she'd added two shoulder pads covered in nasty looking spikes.

"I'm sure they will make short work of it. Even the rogues were able to bypass it with little effort," I replied. Without the proper enchantments and magical protections, the wall that blocked the hall leading to the last level of the dungeon was susceptible to magical lock picks and other relics.

Half an hour passed, then an hour. "Have they left the previous level yet?" I asked.

"I don't believe so," Zarah said.

Curious. Had the wall actually stymied their progress? Such a powerful group should have had little problem with my novice puzzle wall.

Another thirty minutes went by before Zarah spoke. "They've arrived on this level."

We stared down the long hall that led to the exit room. In the distance, the torchlight slowly dimmed as something approached. One by one, the torches went out until darkness engulfed the hall entirely.

"They are here," Xagrim said as three robed figures stepped out from the hall. Thirty feet separated their group from ours. The largest one was about the same size as Xagrim. The next one was my height and build, while the third was about a foot and half shorter than Zarah.

"Greetings, King Therion. We have journeyed far," the shortest member hissed.

"What is it you seek?" I asked.

"You will find out soon enough, fledgling dungeon master."

"W-wait...this seems familiar. I-I recognize them!" Zarah said as fear crept into her voice. "This is the group that defeated the dungeon over a hundred and fifty years ago!"

CHAPTER SEVEN
Fight for Survival

The short one seemed to be the speaker for the group. She chuckled at Zarah's alarm. "I'm surprised to see you survived that encounter, little Dungeon Heart. We thought we had stamped out this dungeon. Imagine our surprise to learn it had not only survived but had recently reopened. I don't know how Orgun managed to save it, but this time we'll make sure the job is finished."

"N-no, that's not possible. You can't still be alive!" Zarah said as she backed away.

"There are many magics in the world. You've seen but a tiny portion of them. It's a pity you shall not see more after today," the leader said as she pointed at the three of us. "Eliminate them. I'll take care of the sphere."

The other two members of the party said in unison, "Through punishment, there is justice."

I noticed the speaker's robe was torn in several spots near the bottom. The arbolisks had indeed almost added another tree to their collection.

"Had a bit of trouble with my pets in the forest?" I asked as we moved to engage the party.

"A slight annoyance, nothing more," the group's leader said as she paused to allow the other two to take the brunt of our attacks.

"*We* will present more than a slight annoyance," I said as I engaged the medium-sized opponent. Xagrim rushed in to attack the largest of them. I was sure that one was their main muscle, but I knew I was wrong as soon as I heard his deep guttural voice muttering a spell.

A geyser of green liquid erupted at Xagrim's feet, coating Xagrim from head to toe. His armor began to sizzle as the powerful acid began to eat away at the outer layers of metal.

"Terrem Hydrososis!" I shouted while gesturing toward Xagrim. The ground at his feet transmuted into water, submerging him completely. His opponent began casting again, this time causing bolts of electricity to cascade across his robes as his spell built in power.

"Oratota Silenci!" I shouted. The counter spell silenced him.

The third opponent leapt toward me, twin curved swords appearing from nowhere. Toxin appeared between us, blocking the two weapons with his twin daggers. The pair quickly squared off, gauging each other's prowess as they looked for weaknesses in their opponent's fighting stance. Each time they clashed, they rebounded back and began circling each other.

I stepped into the path of their leader, my sword and shield readied. She seemed intent on making it into the throne room. Judging by her height, I guessed she must be a gnome or a dwarf. I'd make quick work of her then assist Xagrim with the large spellcaster.

"You're a fool to engage us directly, dungeon master. Do you not understand how this system works?" she said as she flipped back the edge of her cloak to reveal a small sword hilt sheathed in a tiny scabbard. She dashed forward, whipping the blade free and slashing upward at the same time. I instinctively brought my sword up to block her blade, but there was nothing to block.

"What —" I said as something hit my sword with enough force to send me reeling back. My hand stung from the impact. It felt as if I'd tried to deflect a boulder. Yet, I could see no sword in her hand, merely the small hilt.

The small warrior drove forward, taking advantage of my confusion. She swung the small hilt as easily as a feather, but each time I brought up my sword or shield to block, it felt as if Xagrim had unleashed a full-force attack into me. The sheer physical force was battering me into senselessness.

"Jagen!" Zarah called out from the doorway that led to the throne room. She materialized a midnight-black lute and began playing a melody. I felt my muscles bulge and the straps of my armor strain against my flesh.

"This time, we'll eliminate the Dungeon Heart, the Master, and the Soul Sphere," my opponent said upon seeing Zarah.

"This time you'll die," I said as I struck back with Purgatory. Thus far I'd been on the defensive, but it was time to change tactics. Despite my opponent's overwhelming strength and invisible weapon, she was not as good a swordsman as I was. My training with Leath, Xagrim, and Toxin ensured my swordplay could match anyone.

She dodged back, evading my thrusts and swings, blocking them as well as she could. With each parry or block, my perceptions of her weapon's size and makeup increased. It seemed to be a massive great sword, perhaps larger than Xagrim's, with multiple jagged projections from it in order to confuse opponents.

I glanced over to see Xagrim had finally emerged from the pool of water while Toxin flitted in and out of the shadows against his own opponent. Zarah's songs affected all three of us, boosting our strength and stamina. For now, it seemed we held the upper hand. In fact, while our opponents were powerful, they did not seem to be as strong as Leath's group that had previously attacked the dungeon. It was illogical that Ho'Scar and Helatha had fallen so quickly and easily to this party.

A flash of blinding light erupted from Xagrim's direction. A beam of disintegration flowed from the innards of his opponent's robes, striking the death knight squarely in the chest. The spot where the beam impacted began to glow white hot immediately. Noticing my distraction, the small warrior I battled unleashed a devastating attack that sent my sword careening a dozen feet away. I cast one glance at the imperiled death knight before leaping for my sword.

The leader gave chase, jumping into the air and coming down in a vicious double overhand slash that probably would have split me in half if I hadn't rolled to the side at the last minute. Unfortunately for her, she came down in exactly the spot I'd planned when I purposely lost my sword. Magic chains erupted from the invisible trap drawn onto the floor, wrapping around the small warrior's body and weapon. I could now see just how massive the invisible sword was, as well as its basic shape.

Weaving a series of hand signs, I drew a large, complex diagram in the air before sending it toward Xagrim. It paused in front of the embattled knight, intercepting the sizzling magic beam and splitting it into twenty directions. It wasn't the best counter to the spell, but it would prevent Xagrim from melting into slag and give him a moment to recover.

"Do it, now," the leader said as she snapped one of the chains holding her sword.

Xagrim's opponent drew back before unleashing a wave of blinding energy that washed over the entire room. Zarah stopped playing and fell from the air. Toxin reappeared from the shadows and stumbled backward. Xagrim fell to his knees. It felt as if someone had sucked the air from the room. No, the effect was similar to when I'd unleashed my willpower to prevent Zarah from killing Duke Merromont. In fact, the wave of energy felt very similar to...my own energy? How was this possible?

Looking at Xagrim, Toxin, and Zarah, it was as if someone had almost removed the life from them. "What is hap —" I asked before I was forced to dodge the group's leader's sword strike.

"There is no point in wasting the breath to explain it to you," she said as she swung again. I leapt back and ran toward Toxin. Xagrim was durable enough to withstand a bit of punishment before perishing, but Toxin's foe could behead him in seconds in the rogue's current state.

"Multae Ignatous Fragmentum!" I shouted as Toxin's foe bore down on him. Five flame darts flew toward the robed figure. Three hit him — one in the arm, one in the leg, and another in the side. My sigh of relief was short-lived as the enemy continued forward and swatted away Toxin's daggers before impaling him on his twin blades.

Xagrim's opponent had unleashed a spell which created an ominous black cloud above the knight. Red rain fell upon him, causing him to moan in agony. The sound of metal grinding against metal followed, as well as rust spots on his armored form. Still, the giant knight moved forward, his joints creaking and straining against the rust. His opponent backed away slowly, obviously frightened that the knight could still function. However, the spell was one that must be channeled. If he moved too much, it would break his spell.

"Die," Xagrim said as he lunged forward unexpectedly, his massive sword piercing the caster's robe and erupting out of the back. Yet the caster did not jerk or fall or even cease his spell. Xagrim fell again, unable to move from the rust damage to his body.

"What manner of beings are these?" I whispered as Toxin's opponent kicked the limp rogue from his blades and began approaching me. I could feel Toxin yet lived, as did Xagrim. Apparently, it was the enemies' intent to leave my minions alive so that I wouldn't be able to resurrect the pair, hence healing their injuries in the process. They knew much about how the dungeon functioned and used it to their advantage. Xagrim's opponent likewise turned to face me as their leader approached the closed doors to the throne room.

"Jagen!" Zarah called out from just outside the doorway. There was no telling what ominous ability they could utilize against the weakened heart of the dungeon.

"Discorporate, Zarah. It's too dangerous," I said as I watched the caster and dual-sword wielding warrior approach. The Dungeon Heart obediently obeyed and faded away.

"Well, now I don't have to share you with the others," I said as I pointed my sword at the trio.

"Humor in the face of fear. A weakness," the group leader whispered. "Your most powerful minions are defeated. You are outnumbered. It's illogical to continue the battle."

"Yet I see no other way forward," I said as I walked toward the two melee fighters.

"Foolish, human," the dual-sword wielding warrior said as he dove forward. In an instant, the world was a blur as I was blocking the twin blades with my sword and shield. The warrior's blades erupted in fire as the spell caster enhanced them with magic.

I kept close to the warrior as we dueled, continuously forcing him to move about in order to prevent the caster from releasing any spells against me that might hit his companion. At least, that had been the plan. A massive ball of fire lit up my peripheral vision. In the last instant, I brought my shield up to block. The impact smacked me four feet back as the heat and light knocked me senseless. The smell of burnt hair and flesh filled the air. Mentally examining myself, everything seemed to work, but I probably wouldn't know the extent of my injuries until the battle had concluded. For now, the chromatic steel shield had turned a devastating spell into something less.

I now saw why my earlier flame darts had failed. The fireball had burned most of the robe from my melee opponent, revealing his true form. A red-scaled scalax stood before me in

ornate chainmail and leather armor. If I'd used a cold-based attack earlier, Toxin might have been uninjured.

A loud bang from behind me indicated their leader was
attacking the door directly. After several blows, she shouted,
"Bring me the key from the knight."

The caster finished a spell, causing walls of flame to erupt
around the scalax and myself. We were boxed in, and the flames
meant nothing to my opponent. The heat beat against my exposed flesh as we continued our battle. For now, they had taken
me out of the fight as well as my two minions. If they made it
through the door, the Soul Sphere would be vulnerable.

"You've considerable skill for such a young dungeon lord,"
the scalax said as he initiated a dazzling pirouette of blows. His
graceful and powerful movements reminded me much of Zhalix's. In fact, the more we fought, the more I recognized certain
universal elements to their flowing styles of combat and work.

Looking over my current opponent's shoulder revealed the
caster was now a few feet from Xagrim. The knight's incapacitated body began to glow before his hand opened. The key to
the next room appeared and levitated toward the trio's diminutive leader. Xagrim crawled feebly toward the door, still seek-
ing to protect the dungeon despite his current weakened condition.

"How...are you doing this?" I asked feebly as sweat stung
my eyes. "What have you done to my minions?"

"Let's just say — we're something like family," the scalax
said as he unleashed a roundhouse kick that caught me in the
side of my helm. I went with the motion and turned in a full
circle, bringing my sword around as I went down. He leapt over
the blade and I shouted, "Multae Rhymeous Fragmentum!"

Five darts of ice impacted the base of the flaming wall, causing the flames to die down.

The scalax turned to see what I had done, and I rushed in, tackling him in the midsection and carrying the both of us through the weakened flame wall. He brought the hilts of his swords down into my back, but my armor absorbed the blows. My strength far exceeded his own, and he was unable to free himself.

"Xagrim!" I shouted as I slammed the scalax into the pool of water I'd used earlier to save the knight from the acid spell. The death knight rolled over several times and plunged his hand into the pool. His eyes flared as he unleashed his power over the deathly cold. The scalax attempted to leap out, but it was too late. The water solidified around him, encasing him in a solid cylinder of ice. Only his head and one arm outstretched remained above ground.

"I require assistance!" he shouted to his companions.

"Too late," Xagrim said as he brought his heavy gauntlet down on the dragonkin's head. The first blow dented his helmet, and each following dented his skull. After five thunderous fists in a row, he was half a foot shorter than when he'd arrived. Xagrim collapsed from the effort and did not stir.

Panting, I clambered to my feet. The door to the throne room now stood open.

"No!" I shouted as I raced after the last two invaders.

"Stop him," the leader said as she continued into the room. The towering spellcaster turned slowly and began chanting. A wall of barbed blades erupted from the floor, but I vaulted over it before the spell completed. Three fireballs launched one after another, but I slid under them as they sailed overhead. A cloud of glowing green gas appeared, enveloping the entire area in front of the doorway.

"Vortexus Turbini!" I said as I continued forward. The wall of fog parted where the dust devils separated it. The caster attempted yet another spell, but it was too late. Leaping through the air, I lunged at the creature. Purgatory plunged through the front of his robed hood. An inhuman garbled shriek erupted from the caster. Black blood ran down Purgatory's fuller, indicating my attack had been more successful than Xagrim's.

The caster jerked and spasmed, almost ripping Purgatory from my grasp. It shrieked several more times until it fell to the floor — or rather floated. Its cloak deflated as its body seemed to fade away, leaving only its bulbous head remaining. As it came to a rest, the hood of the cloak finally fell away, revealing a large cyclopean head marked by a single large eye and a maw filled with rotted teeth. Its bald skull ended in a pulsing visible brain covered in glowing red veins and arteries that pulsed and thumped. As it died, I felt a weight lifted...as if the creature's power over the dungeon had faded.

A crash that shook the room broke my attention. The leader now stood in front of the Soul Sphere, weapon in hand. I raced across the room, but she'd struck the orb twice more before I could reach her. The sound of glass cracking reverberated through the very walls of the dungeon itself. Zarah's ghostly voice screamed in agony from nowhere.

I brought my sword down, but she whirled and blocked my overhead swing easily. She nodded toward the glowing blue sphere beside us. In its dim light, I could make out some parts of her gnomish face. "It's done," she said triumphantly.

I followed her gaze and a feeling of dread filled me. A small crack now ran from the top of the Soul Sphere to the bottom.

CHAPTER EIGHT
Bleeding

The thin line in the surface of the Soul Sphere glowed a blinding white. My opponent shoved me away as I pondered what the damage to the Soul Sphere meant for the dungeon. "What have you done?"

"Your magic will leak out slowly until there is none left. The sphere can't accumulate new magic. Your dungeon is doomed."

"Can you feel it?" Zarah said as she appeared beside me. "It feels like...my life is ebbing away a fraction at a time."

I pointed my sword at the small warrior. "You'll pay for that."

She laughed as she pulled back the hood of her cloak. She was indeed a gnome, but her skin was ashen and her eyes blood red. How had a gnome become so strong? "I've accomplished my task. While you've defeated my companions, you haven't taken me."

Xagrim creaked as he stepped into the room, seemingly recovered enough to fight. Toxin limped to my side, ready for combat, despite the grievous wounds to his torso. "You forget — whatever ability you used to hamper my minions died with

78

your grotesque companion. How will you fare against the three of us?"

The gnome's smile faded.

SLAMMING THE BOOK CLOSED, I shoved it from my desk and grabbed the next one. There had to be some information about the creature in one of these field manuals.

"What are you going to do about the Soul Sphere?" Zarah asked again.

"I haven't found anything related to fixing it in any book, nor have I been able to identify that creature that depowered you and the others."

"I don't understand what it did to us. It was as if you bent us to your will, ordering us to become complacent and weak. It even felt similar, as if it were coming from you. At first, I thought it was you who had done it."

I turned to face her. "How long until the Sphere is depleted?"

"I don't know. The dungeon itself uses a small amount of power. Killing the intruders refilled it to its maximum, but it seems we can no longer channel the magic from the prisoners into it. I don't believe the Soul Sphere can accept magic again until it's fixed. We are at eighty percent after reviving Ho'Scar, the few goblins who perished, and Helatha. Fortunately for us, the intruders were intent on getting to the Soul Sphere as fast as possible, so most of our minions lived through the ordeal."

"I've asked the Royal Magic Academy for any information they have on this topic, but very little is known about how these places of power function. They seem to operate outside the bounds of known magic and accepted magical theories."

"So, you're just going to read books while the dungeon dies?"

"You have a better suggestion?"

"See if you can contact the artisans again. Yisan or Drundt may know how to fix it."

"I've already done that. They've long left the kingdom, and no one knows where they went. None of the guilds left in the city have any experts on this matter, either. Perhaps if we still had contacts within Inevitable Oblivion, they could find us some underworld artisans or experts, but it seems we've made them angry," I said as I returned to reading through the stack of books that covered half my desk.

"Perhaps it was locking their new leader in the dungeon for weeks?" Zarah suggested.

"She wasn't their leader at the time. We treated them with utmost respect while they were our guests."

"Still...Dusk was pretty furious about that..."

"I make a lot of people furious. If I worried about every person I upset, I'd accomplish nothing. Has Ho'Scar uncovered anything from the gnome?"

"Not yet. He says he needs to nurse her back to health a bit because the three of you almost beat her to death. Then he can begin the proper torture methods."

"Have one of the younger shamans assist in the healing process. We need to know everything possible about these new intruders. Have Xagrim and Toxin healed completely yet? Has the damage to the Soul Sphere interfered with the process?"

"They are healing, albeit it slightly slower than normal. Another day and they should be in top form. I've played my rejuvenation songs for them several times, which seemed to help."

"Good. We need our defenses at the ready in case there are more of these invaders."

"You have a visitor," Zarah said as she looked toward the door.

"I heard you had quite a battle, son," Leath said.

"Indeed. A party unlike any we've seen before. They were able to circumvent our defenses by means of a spell or unknown ability of some kind. I wanted to ask you if you've ever come across anything like that in your travels. It was as if our minions were universally weakened or made subservient to the intruders as they progressed through the dungeon."

Leath rubbed his burgeoning salt-and-pepper beard. "Other than paralysis, sleep, stun, and similar mental-type spells, I've not heard of anything like that. Perhaps it was a powerful artifact?"

"No, Publin and I looked over their weapons and armor. I found nothing unusual...except for this," I said as I held out a small glowing orb.

"Well, perhaps this is what did it? I've seen smaller enchanted objects," Leath said as he marveled at the gleaming sphere.

"No, Publin said it seems to be a container of some sort, not a weapon or tool. As far as I can tell, it merely holds magic. Perhaps an exterior storage system to replenish magical reserves. The unusual thing is I found this on their warrior, not their mage. Speaking of which, have you ever seen a creature such as this before?" I asked as I stood and moved to a nearby table, removing a heavy cloth from the corpse.

"By the gods! That's what that stench was!" Leath exclaimed as he brought an arm up to cover his nose. He leaned in to examine the monster. "It looks like a small cyclops' head to me. Where's the rest of him? If he smells like this, I hope you burned it. Looks like you bashed its brains out."

"This is all there was of him. Simply a floating head giving the illusion of a large man's body underneath. The mutations such as the enlarged cranium and exposed brain are inherent to the creature, not the result of an injury."

"No, perhaps some type of necromancy, although not any I've seen outside of..."

"Outside of what?"

"Outside of a dungeon such as this. I've seen many aberrations of nature over the years. Twisted fiends and devious monstrosities, but they rarely occur in nature. They are created in places...such as your dungeon."

"You're saying you believe these are creatures from a place of power or a dungeon?" I asked as I stared at the monstrous head. That could explain the gnome's immense strength as well.

"Yet, dungeon creatures are unable to leave their dungeons. They must be near the dungeon's heart in order to maintain...life," I said as I turned back to my desk. The small glowing orb was filled with pure magic. "Unless this is actually..."

"You think that's some kind of Soul Sphere?" Zarah asked as she appeared beside the desk.

"Perhaps," I said as I picked the object up and attempted to draw from its power. The magic felt familiar. Similar to the magic that flowed through our dungeon, but it had a dis-tinct...flavor to it. The magic wouldn't come to me.

"Yes, I believe this allowed these creatures to travel from another dungeon to ours without any negative side effects. They came right through the front gate and attacked us just as any adventurer's party would have."

"Yes, we lost ten good men when they did so. I had no idea your dungeon would draw such powerful enemies," Leath said. "I've doubled the guard with my best men. Some of which have experience dealing with such matters. I hate to take them away from securing the city, but your security matters most. I feel like I've failed you by allowing these creatures to attack."

"You can't be in two places at once, and I need you in the city. This was a powerful group, but the real threat was their ability to incapacitate my minions. We must find out how they were able to do that."

"I think the best way to do that is to ask her yourself," Zarah said. "Of course, she'll have to regain consciousness first."

THE SHAMAN AND HO'SCAR had done an exemplary job healing our newest prisoner. Stitches and bandages covered much of her visible flesh, but she would make a full recovery in time. We had been perhaps a bit zealous in our retribution.

"She's a strange one. Almost stronger than me, and that's sayin' somethin'. Little shit broke two of my fingers while I was fixin' 'er up. Never heard of a gnome that strong. Ain't natural.

Fact is, she reminds me a bit o' Toxin. I'm not real sure if she's alive or dead. Somethin' in-between, I'd say," Ho'Scar said as he led us to the gnome.

"What are those strange nodules in her skull?" I asked. It almost looked as if something had been implanted under her skin.

"Beats the hells out of me. Only thing I got out of 'er so far is her name, which she says is Sheet Branes. Weird name if'n you ask me," the torturer said.

Zarah and I shared a bemused glance. "And what is her middle name?" Zarah asked.

"You 'eard the lady, what's yer middle name?" Ho'Scar asked as he prodded the chained gnome with a sharp poker.

She looked up and smiled. "Fer. It was my grandmother's name."

"You wish to be difficult. That's fine...my torturer has all the time in the world," I said.

Ho'Scar scratched his head. "Sheet Fer Branes. Is that a Mangorian name?" Zarah stifled a laugh.

"I don't think your torturer has as much time as you think. Neither do you. Your Soul Sphere is damaged, and you'll all be dead in a matter of days. Perhaps a week at the most," the gnome sneered.

"Who sent you? Why did you attack us? How did you overcome my minions?"

The gnome closed her mouth and stared at the ceiling.

"I could let you go if you cooperate. Surely freedom would be preferable to torture and death?" I offered.

She laughed. "My master's torture chamber makes this crude room look like a brothel."

"You admit you were sent by a rival dungeon lord to strike at our heart. How does the sphere we found on you work?"

"You'll never find out before you're dead," the gnome replied.

"At least tell us your name," Zarah said.

The gnome ceased speaking entirely.

"Do what you can, Ho'Scar, but be careful — this prisoner is unlike any you've encountered thus far. She may have some hidden abilities or some such," I said.

"Aye, that's why I got that collar on 'er. Blocks 'er access to magic, same as any caster that comes in 'ere. Can't have 'em shoutin' spells and whatnot," Ho'Scar said as he measured the gnome with a piece of twine. "Blasted gnomes are too small fer most of the machines, but I figure I got a few that'll do the trick."

"What do we do next?" Zarah asked once we were outside.

"I didn't expect to gain much information from her. At least we know she was sent by a rival dungeon lord, although why they would attack us is a mystery," I said. "It can't have anything to do with a personal grudge against me, because they also attacked Orgun. Therefore, the reason must lie in the dungeon itself."

"Maybe they don't like competition?" Zarah suggested.

"Perhaps. Although I would guess there are more than enough adventurers and prisoners to satisfy a multitude of dungeons and other places of power."

"Maybe they just want our loot?"

"I doubt it. This group seemed only interested in destroying the dungeon, not the wealth."

Upon returning to the throne room, I noticed Publin sitting in front of the Soul Sphere with a dozen open books scattered about. "Have you any idea on how to repair the damage?"

He looked up from a book, startled by our arrival. "I-I don't even know what this is...some kind of magical siphon and storage device...but how does it work? What's it made of? Who built it?"

"I have the answer to none of your questions, and the fact you are asking me those questions indicates you have no idea how to repair it, correct?" I said.

"I...wish I did, but this is beyond me. It might even be beyond the master wizards at the academy. I've never heard of anyone studying a wondrous artifact such as this."

"So, you weren't able to gain assistance from any of the guilds or the academy?" I asked bluntly.

"N-no. The guilds say your dungeon is a place of evil, and the academy has been...stonewalling me."

"I am the King of Tharune, and I've issued a direct order for the heads of the Royal Magic Academy to attend to me, and you say they are...stonewalling?"

"I'm just a novice enchanter, I don't have any power..."

The veins in my head began to throb. "Where is Leath? He should be able to force some action on this matter!"

"You sent him into the city to quell a food riot," Zarah said.

"Blast it! Why is it I have an entire nation and dungeon at my disposal yet I'm continually without the help I need? Must I do everything myself?"

"Because you pissed off every powerful person you've come across and all of them want to see you fail?" Zarah offered.

She'd disappeared before I could turn around and issue a retort.

CHAPTER NINE
A Voice in the Darkness

The beautiful dream was the same one I'd enjoyed dozens of times. Despite Helatha's interference, it remained unsullied. Aiyla and myself on a cool night in Nosteran, just the two of us. Our bodies' warmth kept the chill desert winds at bay. The night air flowing throughout the room, causing the candles and lamps to flicker and dance — giving us yet another reason to seek each other's embrace.

Yet something else intruded into the dream. A feeling of dread...of need. Something was amiss, yet I couldn't determine the source of the concern clawing at the back of my mind. Going to the window, I surveyed the moonlit dunes as the desert winds howled.

"It is time," a voice called out from the darkness. A force ripped me from the room, sending me flailing from the window. I grasped for anything to save myself, but the ground rushed to meet me with a sickening thud. Darkness followed.

Jerking awake, I gasped for air. The light level from the magical orbs increased slightly in response to my movement. The need to relieve myself forced me out from my sweat-drenched blankets. Drundt had mentioned the possibility of installing a system of waterways powered by the underground streams that ran through the surrounding area that would eliminate the need for the chamber pots. He stated the dwarves had perfected such systems centuries ago, but it was a time-and-labor intensive process and dungeon repairs had taken precedence. Perhaps when they'd become free from the dungeon's influences, he could return and implement such luxuries.

I froze as the hairs on the back of my neck stood on end. I sensed that I wasn't alone. My sword was on the other side of the room. I finished my business then slowly inched to the side, ready to dive at the first hint of an attack. The feeling that something was watching me increased. I thought of calling out to Zarah. Perhaps her sudden appearance would startle the intruder long enough for me to reach my weapon.

"Multae Illuminous Manifestae!" I shouted as I dashed forward while aiming the spell over my shoulder. The room exploded with light as a half dozen blinding orbs of light erupted behind me. Reaching my sword, I whirled to find...nothing. The room was empty. I checked around the bookcases, shower, under the bed, and looked out into the silent throne room. The Soul Sphere's dim blue light provided the only illumination, but there was nothing unusual. Dispelling the annoyingly bright orbs, I sat on the edge of the bed.

My instincts had led me astray for the first time I could remember. Perhaps the unnatural recent attack had unnerved me. Setting my sword beside the bed, I pulled back the blankets and gasped. I grabbed and unsheathed my sword and shouted, "Show yourself! I know I'm not alone!" Quickly, I inspected the room again to find the intruder but found nothing.

"Zarah."

She appeared instantly, looking over the situation with amusement. "A nightmare? Did Helatha try to seduce you again?"

"No. I felt a presence, but I wasn't able to locate an intruder. Then I returned to my bed to find...this," I said as I pointed to the object which laid perfectly centered in the bed.

"Orgun's staff? Are you sure you didn't bring it in here and fall asleep with it in your bed?" Zarah said as she yawned.

"I'm positive. Yet here it is," I said as I grabbed the staff.

"Time is short," a hollow-sounding whisper said.

"Did you hear that?" I asked.

Zarah looked around and shook her head. "It's too late in the night for you to go insane, Jagen. Why don't you get some rest and perhaps —"

Suddenly, I was somewhere else. I now stood in a massive room. Thousands of books lined the walls as a spiral staircase wound its way higher and higher along the walls. I was at the base of the structure on the ground floor. Complicated contraptions and mystical artifacts floated and glowed all about, some with electricity dancing around them, while others periodically vented fire. Several tables around the room held various alchemical implements, such as glass beakers and test tubes. Complex magical and mathematical formulae were scrawled across massive slate boards near the various projects.

Moving about the room, I attempted to ascertain the purpose of each project. Glancing at the notes on the board as well as a few open notebooks, my tired mind reeled at the possibilities.

I attempted to identify three skeletons against the wall before noticing a floating display of rotating spheres levitating fifty feet above the floor.

"Orgun's inner sanctum..." I whispered as my mind leapt from one spectacle to the next.

"You are here sooner than I'd planned, but your foolishness left me little choice," the voice I'd heard before said.

I looked at the staff clenched tight in my sweaty palms. "You are the one speaking to me."

"Your dungeon is fatally damaged, and you sleep comfortably in your bed dreaming of that wench. It's appalling! You should be doing whatever is necessary to save the dungeon, fool!"

"How is it you possess intelligence and speak?" I asked.

"You will have a thousand questions, and you will wish to indulge in Orgun's experimentations and notes. Your mind is too infantile to understand the concepts of these studies. It would take you decades to begin to comprehend the majority of these wonders. You have one goal in your miserable life at this moment — save the dungeon," the voice said.

"I..." I began to say as I caught a glimpse of what looked like a fractured Soul Sphere.

"Yes, that's the sphere they damaged on their first attack on the dungeon. Orgun crafted the one which adorns your throne room."

"Then there is a way to craft a new one. Tell me where his notes are concerning this and I will begin work immediately," I said. My mind reeled from the wonders all around me. I then realized I was carrying on a conversation with a stick.

"Yes, of course there is a way, buffoon! If it was created once, it can be created again! The problem lies in the fact you do not re-

motely possess the skills to do so; you also do not have the basic ma-terials."

"Simply tell me what I must do. I have an entire kingdom at my disposal. I will obtain these materials and hire experts to help me construct —"

"You will do as I say. Your dungeon is doomed unless you follow my directions. I brought you here because the various en-chantments in this room allow us to communicate directly with-out effort. They are intended to open the mind to possibilities and remove negative thoughts and blockades to knowledge."

Such enchantments sounded dangerous. Orgun had proved he could easily manipulate my memories, and now mind-altering magics swirled throughout the room. My thirst for knowledge had been rekindled, but was it the work of the strange magic surrounding us? In fact, the dungeon and Tharune seemed like distant worries not worthy of my atten-tion. The desire to remain in the sanctum and work on the various projects strewn about the laboratory was becoming stronger.

"Is that a Mangorian sand spider skull?" I said as something caught my attention. Even the Royal Mage Academy didn't have —

"Focus on my voice. The skull is not of importance. Remember your dungeon. Remember the damaged Soul Sphere. Remem-ber...Zarah," the staff commanded.

The skull didn't matter. Nothing in the room mattered ex-cept repairing the dungeon.

"What did you do?" I asked. Was the staff controlling my thoughts?

"I served my primary purpose. To pull you away from the magics in this room and your own curiosity. Otherwise you would become so infatuated with study you'd die from lack of food and rest."

"Who are you? Are you the soul of some lost mage bound to the staff? Some type of artifact given a rudimentary intelligence?"

"I will reveal that in time. For now, know you can trust me. I brought you here so that we can discuss the dungeon. Unfortunately, for now, this is the only place you will be able to freely communicate with me, due to the mind-expanding magics placed upon the sanctum. I do not relish constantly dragging your mind away from the myriad distractions in this room, however. It was exhausting even with Orgun, and your mind is far younger than his."

"It is...difficult to focus on your words, but if you have information that will save the dungeon, you must tell me," I said as I eyed a strange metal man slumped over in a corner. Was it some type of golem? It appeared to be of gnomish design...

"Listen to me, fool! Stop fawning over worthless junk! Your dungeon can be saved, but you must act quickly. You've wasted enough time bumbling around attempting to gain assistance from the guilds and the Academy. You won't find the answers to your questions through traditional channels. These places of power do not operate on the same principles as standard magic. Given a few years at your current skill level, you might be able to create another Soul Sphere. Instead, you will have to find another before your dungeon dies."

"Another? Tell me where it is, and I will send Leath and a battalion to retrieve it, no matter where it may lie," I said. "Is it in Mangoria? Nosteran? The Land of Death?"

The staff mentally chuckled. "*While there are indeed Soul Spheres and similar constructs in dungeons and old places in those lands, the one you seek is right beneath your feet. It is buried deep beneath your throne room.*"

"Beneath...but Drundt said it was impossible to tunnel deeper below the dungeon. Powerful magics prevent it."

"*Aye. The same magics that make it impossible to tunnel between floors of your dungeon. You see, your dungeon is merely the top of an ancient structure that runs much deeper into the depths. If you wish to save it, you will need to reclaim the lost levels below...if you can.*"

CHAPTER TEN

A New Quest

Zarah looked at me in disbelief. "You say Orgun's staff told you this? I don't recall him ever mentioning it could talk. Are you sure you're feeling okay? Perhaps a fever..."

"No, I was in Orgun's inner sanctum. It was filled with such wondrous...knowledge..." I said as my mind drifted away to what I'd seen. I wanted to go back immediately.

Zarah snapped her fingers to regain my attention. "I would think I would know if the dungeon contained another Soul Sphere. I *have* been here over one and a half centuries."

"Yet you said Orgun rarely spoke with you or interacted with the daily dungeon duties. In the end, you were basically alone."

"Yes...that's true. I don't know what he was doing in that room of his. As I said, I wasn't allowed entry, and I've never seen it. It seemed he only told me what I needed to know," Zarah said as she soothingly strummed a harp.

"The staff stated I needed to assemble a strong party to venture below. The danger lies in the fact the levels below may have fallen into disrepair and grown wild over these many years," I said as I began flipping through a notebook Carine had left me which contained the current members of her adventurers' guild. Without knowing the exact dangers we'd be facing, it would be difficult to gather a worthy party from her current roster of adventurers.

"Did the staff give you any details on these supposed floors?" Zarah asked.

"It told me the basics of what they used to be, long ago. Orgun found it impossible to continue his experimentations and study while maintaining so many floors. The magic requirements were too great. So, he left the bottom floors to rot and built a new Soul Sphere on this level. A small dungeon requires less maintenance and magic."

"It seems he basically did the same with the upper floors after the first attack by this group. Perhaps he could have repaired the dungeon and reopened the entrance, but he chose to place me in a suspended state and let the dungeon fend for itself," Zarah said with a hint of resentment in her voice.

Had he retired to his sanctum to research something to the detriment of the dungeon and Zarah? Perhaps in doing so, he'd cost himself the eternal life he might have otherwise enjoyed if the dungeon had thrived. Perhaps the sanctum had caused him to become so addicted he was unable to focus on the dungeon's daily needs. What knowledge could have been worth sacrificing so much?

"We will need supplies. Ropes, rations, torches, medical supplies," I said as I closed the book. Only one person from the listings would possibly be worthwhile for my expedition — yet I was hesitant to remove her from her duties, such as they were.

"I'll see to your list. Will you select Leath to travel with you?"

Leath was a veteran of many such missions and would be an invaluable resource, but while the city was still in turmoil, it needed a strong leader. I didn't know how long the expedition would take, and New Vadis would suffer if both Leath and I were gone for too long. Kurth's exceptional organization skills had been a boon over the past few weeks, but he lacked the raw force to make men do his bidding.

"No. Send Leath a message that I will be indisposed for a while, and he is to assume rule of the city in my stead. Make sure he understands no one else is to know I will be gone."

"It will be done," Zarah said as she jotted everything down on her magical parchment before drawing the floating instrument back to her.

"And you will have to assume control of the dungeon," I said.

Zarah froze. "I...you want me to —"

"Is that a problem? You've done it before and are more than capable."

Zarah let her instrument fade away. "It's just...with that group...I felt powerless. Like this fear had come over me that I never wanted to experience again. When they almost killed me all those years ago, and then to see them again. I was so terrified it was like I didn't know what to do. I don't think I could face that again by myself."

I crossed the room and stood behind her. "The staff says I'm the only one who can save the dungeon. I'll have to find the Soul Sphere below and activate it before this one runs out of magic. We will both need to face our fears if we are to succeed."

Zarah turned to face me, disbelief in her voice and on her face. "You? When have you been afraid? You face every challenge without hesitation."

"I've been afraid since I've set foot in the dungeon. Afraid I wouldn't survive. Afraid of the rogues. Afraid of my father. Yet I've always moved forward because there is no alternative. Dwelling on what may happen or could have happened is a waste of time. You've overcome every threat you've faced in your life and persevered, just as I have. You are also almost ten times older than I am, so that means you've got far more experience in dealing with problems," I said with a smile.

"I will make sure to wake you up with the biggest drum I can imagine for the rest of your days..." she replied.

"I take it back! I'm just trying to lighten your mood, but jokes are not my expertise. I will just say I trust you utterly with the dungeon."

"I wish I had your confidence. Regardless, we have no choice, so I have to do my best," Zarah said with resignation.

"I'll make sure Leath provides the utmost security for the exterior of the dungeon while I'm gone. We'll close the entrance as well. Until I return, the dungeon will be sealed off from the outside world."

"We might as well. It's not like we are gaining magic from adventurers or the prisoners while the Soul Sphere is cracked. Wait...how will you travel away from the Sphere? You know you grow weaker the farther you are from it. The lower levels won't be connected to the dungeon," Zarah said.

"Ah. Our friends left us a means to accomplish that," I said as I held out the small orb we'd confiscated from the gnome.

LEATH PACED THE THRONE room. "Are you sure this is the way, son?" Once he heard I was leaving, he had demanded to hear what I intended.

"I see no other path. I need to take a group below in order to secure another sphere or the dungeon will perish."

"We could try to bring in experts to remove your link to the dungeon, like we suggested before."

"Leath, we were unable to secure even a proper enchanter. What makes you believe we will be able to garner the help of the most powerful magic users in the country? I admit I was too forceful once assuming control of the city. Now the city is half empty and I can get no support from the outside. We are on our own for now."

"At least let me come with you. There's no telling what you may face down there."

"No. Assume control of the city and continue serving as you have. It could finish ripping itself apart without a central figure to guide it," I said.

"Son, I've told you I'm not that man. Politics and meetings aren't why I was put on Derode. Missions like this is. It's in my blood."

"Perhaps another time, old friend. The people need their hero right now. If I don't succeed, someone will need to rule until my family can be found."

"You sound as if you don't intend on returning from this quest, Jagen. Is there something you aren't telling me?"

"No. I simply plan for every contingency. I don't have much experience in exploring places such as this. This is a list of supplies I plan on bringing. Do you have any old friends who you can recommend? We could use a veteran healer."

Leath looked over the list. "I've known two great healers over the years. One's retired and the other's dead. After you locked up or drove out most of the high-ranking members of the Uxper Orthodoxy, I don't think you'll find many willing to help you in the city, either."

"I'll have to continue with my contingency plan, then. The dungeon is not without its own resources."

"Who are you going with, if you don't mind my asking?"

"If what Orgun's staff says is true, I can purge the portable sphere we recovered from the gnome and fill it with this dungeon's magic. I'll then be able to take Xagrim, Toxin, one of the goblin shamans, and...Carine with me."

"The Taste of Adventure guild leader? The gnome? Why would you take her?"

"Because she actually has a bit of dungeon experience and is a technical expert on contraptions and mechanisms. While Toxin is an expert at lock picking and traps, she may be of some use in other areas. If he were still here, I might have considered taking Drundt."

"Can you trust her?" Leath asked as he grabbed a quill and began writing a few notes on the parchment.

"I believe so. I've had all of the new city leaders under additional surveillance for the past few weeks and nothing leads me to believe she is working for any outside agencies or factions."

"Why her? I haven't heard of any outstanding deeds or anything to make me believe she would be qualified for this quest.

This isn't the time to break in someone new, son. You want people you can count on."

"My group will be made up of minions from the dungeon. I'd like to have at least one companion from outside. The recent attack on the dungeon has made it clear that there are forces I do not understand in play and that I may not be able to count on my servants when I need them most."

"Well, you can count on me. I'll personally pick the men to guard the dungeon entrance from the Royal Guard. I've drawn up plans to place regiments of soldiers around the city and in the forest as well. Based on what you told me of the skill and power of this last group, we will be able to handle anything that comes calling while you are away."

"You can count on me as well, Master," Helatha said as she entered.

"Helatha, I did not call for you. I do not want to strip the dungeon of all of its most powerful defenders," I said.

"I've failed you twice, now, and I wish to make amends. Your group contains sufficient might but is lacking in mystical power. While you've grown in your magical abilities, you'd still be described as a journeyman in terms of your skill level. I can offer both spellcasting and blessings and curses to the party," the soul snatcher said with confidence.

"She's right, son. You're certainly no full-fledged wizard, and she's got decades of experience on you," Leath said.

While I'd considered Helatha for the group, her...affections for me had caused me to cross her off the list. I didn't want a member in the group whose judgment could be clouded by their feelings. She was the most powerful caster in the dungeon, yet also one of the most ruthless.

"I'm not sure if —" I began to say before Zarah walked in, followed by one of the goblin shamans.

"And here is your healer for the group. Gogbog, one of the senior shamans of the goblin tribe," the Dungeon Heart announced.

"Senior" was one way of describing the elder shaman. Decrepit was another. He looked as if he would have trouble with the stairs, much less any threats we encountered. I started to offer an objection, but the shaman held up his hand.

"Allow speak. Shaman held counsel with spirits. Vision appear and showed Gogbog and others that Gogbog must go with Master deep into the ground."

"You saw us undertaking this quest? That there are more levels to the dungeon?" I asked.

The elder shaman nodded. "Spirits showed us. Very important Gogbog go."

Leath chuckled. "I don't think you can argue with the spirits."

I wondered what else the spirits could show us. Orgun's staff outlined what each level had contained in the distant past, but it also cautioned that things could have changed drastically since then. Perhaps the shaman's spirits could guide us.

"Gogbog and Helatha will both accompany us into the dungeon's depths. Prepare yourselves. The dungeon is dying, and we must make haste if we are to save it and ourselves."

CHAPTER ELEVEN
Level Eight

The hastily gathered group before me did not inspire confidence. A spell casting cleric of Castigous, who was actually a soul snatcher, inhabiting the stolen body of a cleric of Uxper. An undead rogue who had been the former guild leader of Inevitable Oblivion. A towering emotionless death knight who reveled in death and despair. An elderly goblin shaman hooked into a rickety harness latched to Xagrim's back. Carine Mordu, the diminutive talkative gnomish leader of the adventurer's guild, Taste of Adventure.

While the group had sufficient power and abilities, it lacked the most important factor for success — teamwork and experience. A vision of Xagrim unleashing a sweeping blow that decapitated Carine flashed into my mind.

"Wish I could come along," Zarah said as she looked over the crew. She paused to regard Carine. "It should be good for a laugh either way."

"I think we have too many members already, but I appreciate your enthusiasm," I said as I fished the small orb that we'd taken from the intruders out of a pouch. Kneeling down to the

Penance of Fate, I dipped it into the sanguine liquid. The magic contained within the sphere drained away, leaving a completely translucent orb. The staff's instructions had worked thus far — now for the most crucial step. Tapping the artifact to the side of the Soul Sphere, I willed the magic to flow between the two spheres. A moment later, the larger orb had been drained of one-eight of its remaining magic while the portable sphere was now filled completely.

"Oh, this should be marvelous — running the dungeon by myself with even less magic," Zarah said.

"You have an entire army protecting Old Vadis and specifically the dungeon entrance. If the next group is stronger than our army, we would be helpless to stop them regardless," I said.

"I have the remnants of your leftover army. The real army is in Nosteran," Zarah argued.

"My point stands. Everyone remain silent — I must focus," I said as I held the staff out and synced my will and magic to it. While I ruled the dungeon now, Orgun had used the staff to permanently seal the entrance to the exit leading down. I would require the staff's assistance and guidance to open it. I closed my eyes.

"Yes...lend me your magic, dungeon lord..." the staff whispered in my mind as it tugged at my consciousness. *"There is your door. Do not call upon me again until you have managed to secure the next Soul Sphere. If you are not capable of that simple feat, you are unworthy of my attention."* Its voice faded away as the mental link broke abruptly.

Opening my eyes revealed a glowing white dot which appeared on the bottom of the wall several feet to the left of the Soul Sphere. The dot moved vertically, leaving a blazing trail behind it on the gleaming black stone. Slowly, it traced the out-line of a door. Once it met back at its origin point, a keyhole appeared with a midnight-black key already lodged in the mechanism.

"Fancy!" Zarah said.

Grabbing the key, I turned it, which resulted in the door pushing out and sliding to the side, revealing a stairwell leading into darkness. I then handed the heavy key to a nearby goblin guard. "Place this in my study in a locked chest." While I was confident that we would have no intruders while away, I didn't trust the goblins with the key. It would probably end up in the bottom of the Penance of Fate or in someone's belly during a drinking contest.

"I've checked over our supplies, and we are ready to explore, oh great leader!" Carine said with far too much enthusiasm.

"I...thank you for your service. Just so there are no misunderstandings — Toxin and Xagrim will take point together. Toxin will search for any threats and traps while Xagrim will absorb the brunt of any surprise attacks. I'll follow Xagrim and provide additional protection and assistance for Gogbog. Helatha and Carine will bring up the rear and provide cover fire and support spells and hexes."

"Are you sure you have to lead this?" Zarah asked. "If you die, then it's the end of everything. Dungeon Masters are supposed to let their minions do the work."

"Who among those assembled would be able to hold this group together?" I asked.

Carine jumped up and down with her hand raised.

Ignoring the gnome, I continued, "Only I can. It's the only way," I said as I checked over my belongings one more time. "We are wasting time. The Soul Sphere loses magic by the minute. Begin the descent," I said, pointing down the stairwell. Toxin faded from view, and Xagrim clanked loudly onto the first step. The massive metal death knight apparently did not have a stealth setting. I summoned two globes of light and Carine lit a torch.

The dusty steps hadn't been used in well over one hundred years. There was no evidence of any activity. An earthy smell began the permeate the air the lower we descended. Toxin met us in the landing room at the base of the steps.

"I've found no immediate traps, but scouting will be a problem," the rogue said as he nodded toward the door.

Glancing out the door, I could see what he meant. Vast caverns sprawled ahead of us, stalactites and stalagmites dozens of feet long erupted from the floors and ceiling like massive teeth from some ancient leviathan. Glowing crystals in the walls and ceilings provided an eerie dim light consisting of various shades of blues and greens.

"It's beautiful!" Carine said as she stepped into the room and twirled about.

"It's an annoyance," Helatha said as she moved out of the landing room. "There's no telling where the key to the next level would be or if the magics even function after so long. Did the staff state what enemies we may face?"

"It was once inhabited by a few dozen trained psuthals. Most likely the one I encountered on level one somehow worked its way up from this level. The creatures are very flexible due to the fact much of their body is made up of cartilage and their joints are reversible. It's how they manage to slip through crevices and travel through the underground with ease," I said as we moved ahead warily.

Helatha made a dismissive motion with her hand. "I was concerned we would face more powerful threats as we journeyed deeper."

"We don't know what we face. I expect many of these levels will now be abandoned, as they have been cut off from food supplies and magic for over a century. If we are lucky, we simply need to make our way down to the next Soul Sphere, where I can reactivate it," I said.

"That sounds extremely boring. I hope we at least run into a giant or a dragon!" Carine complained.

"Why would a dragon or giant be living underground with no access to the outside world? Why did you bring this annoyance, Master?" Helatha said.

"There will be no squabbling on this mission. Carine has certain abilities and tools I believe will be useful. She would not be here if I did not wish it."

Helatha cast a withering glance at the gnome. "As you say, Master. But this level is massive. How will we locate the key?"

"We can't be completely sure this level even has a key. These sections of the dungeon have been abandoned so long; I would be surprised if the keys and doors remain linked or even exist."

"And that's where I come in," Carine said as she removed a device from her satchel. It had a handle with a triangle-shaped panel on the end, with several dials and a needle that could move back and forth across a color-coded range that went from red to green. She pulled out two expandable antennae from the end.

"I call it the Key Zoomer Two-Thousand. If there's a key on this level, this'll help us find it," Carine said as she fiddled with several of the dials.

"This is why you brought her along?" Helatha said with disdain.

"Silence, Helatha. Do you detect anything, Carine?" I asked. If we could head directly to the keys on each level, we could avoid any unnecessary battles or traps — just as the invading group had just done on the upper levels. I still wasn't sure how they'd done that, but it most likely had to do with the mutated cyclops entity. If we returned from this adventure, I intended to bring the remnants to Orgun's sanctum for further study.

"First, we have to sync the dungeon's magic to the Key Zoomer. Usually I do this as we kill monsters and their magic escapes, but in this instance..." she said as she held the device out toward me.

I grasped the antennae and let the dungeon's magic flow into the device as she continued to work the dials. "Got it. That's a much faster method, don't you think? Aha! I've got a reading." She began sweeping the device back and forth until the needle moved into the green area of the display. "If there's a key, it's gotta be this way." She motioned for Xagrim and I to step forward. "After you, gentlemen."

Xagrim grunted at the accusation. "I don't believe he enjoys being called gentle," I said as we took the lead.

The massive caverns loomed all about us as we moved forward. I kept my orbs weak so as to avoid throwing too much light, which resulted in the space around us leading into utter darkness at the edges of the light. We could only see an area roughly ten to fifteen feet in any direction. Despite my caution, I had a feeling we would appear as a blinding beacon to anything lurking just outside our range of vision.

"I feel like a moving target," Carine whispered.

I nodded. "Better than a sitting target. We should remain quiet. Many of these subterranean creatures are sensitive to vibrations and noise."

"I can't be making more noise than the giant death knight," Carine argued.

Each step Xagrim took sounded like a spoon banging on a pot. He was oblivious to the noise, simply striding forth like an animated statue.

"If we had a proper enchanter, we could have created plates to go on the bottom of his feet to deaden the noise. Unfortunately, we have to proceed with the resources we have," I explained. We needed the large armored warrior to provide cover for the group. Leath had long ago explained that two or three warriors were ideal for a group such as this, so that they could protect the weaker members from the front and rear.

"I feel life here, but it is impossible to determine the direction or numbers," Helatha said. "It could be merely natural wildlife, or...something else."

We continued to plod through the cavern for what could have been two miles. The wet, clay floor squished underneath our feet at times, while at others it hardened into firm stone. We had to travel around many rocky growths, which delayed our progress. At one point, a massive column rose into the air, disappearing into the darkness. It had to have been a hundred feet in diameter.

"Fascinating growths. I wonder what minerals compose many of them," I said as I observed a stalagmite that swirled with glowing blue and red colors.

"I wonder what they taste like?" Carine said as she sniffed one. "I've heard some of these glowing minerals taste like sugar rock."

"Please do not tax our healers so early in the mission," I warned as she pulled her tongue away.

Occasionally, Toxin would reappear on our flanks and walk with us for a short period before disappearing back into the shadows. It was reassuring to know the experienced rogue was keeping tabs on us.

"Are any of you feeling any side effects of being away from the upper dungeon? Weaker or more vulnerable?" I asked.

"Nay," Xagrim said.

"No...although I feel the need to be nearer to you, now," Helatha said as she moved slightly closer during the walk.

It seemed the portable sphere I now carried served as the power source for the companions who were linked to the dungeon. Would this mean that once we returned, I would be able to walk among the people of New Vadis? That I could stand atop a mountain and watch the sun rise? What of Zarah? Would she still be tethered to the Soul Sphere in the throne room? I wish we'd had more time to experiment with the new artifact we'd taken from the invaders, but Orgun's staff had been quite vehement about finding a new power source for the dungeon.

"Is it time for a break yet?" Carine asked. "Feels like we've been walking for hours."

"Time is running out. We will have to keep rest periods to a minimum. We will only break if it is necessary to replenish our magic, sleep, or heal," I said.

"I could...use a small respite," Helatha said. Sweat glistened on her forehead and she was having trouble keeping up with the group. Toxin and Xagrim needed no rest, and I was in peak physical shape, but I hadn't considered what such a physically draining trek would do to the others. Even Gogbog seemed tired, despite merely riding Xagrim the entire time.

"Very well, we will take a short break," I said as I pointed toward a flat, open area.

"Thank Zoustero!" Carine said as she plopped down and removed her pack.

I set my own bag down and leaned against a rock formation. Helatha sat beside me and pulled out a bit of cured meat and wine and handed them to me.

I took a bite and a swig before handing back the wineskin. "Thank you, Helatha."

"I live to serve you, Master," she said with a smile. "In any way you wish."

"You..." I began to say before realizing I didn't know how to answer. Her devotion was reassuring but also concerning. Fortunately, Carine broke up the awkward situation.

"Say, any of you have a ruby?" she asked as she fiddled with another device.

Helatha's smile faded. "No."

"I neglected to pack gemstones," I said.

"Oh, well, I'll fix it when we get back," the gnome said as she stowed the device in a magical bag.

"Perhaps we will find one on our adventure," Helatha said with dripping sarcasm.

"Do you really think so? That's one reason I come down into these places. I'd never be able to afford all the components I need on my own, but you never know what might turn up in a dungeon or abandoned tower. Once I found this piece of elvish glass that was probably three hundred years old. You can't even buy that *anywhere.* It has such remarkable refractive properties in comparison to —"

"Please stop speaking," Helatha said as she massaged her forehead.

"You know, I get that a lot. People simply have no interest in the mechanical properties of ancient materials these days," Carine said defensively.

I had honestly been curious to hear more about the properties of the glass, but, in the interest of keeping the peace, I didn't press the issue. I wondered if Carine could assist in the various projects strewn about Orgun's laboratory and sanctum...or if there was even a way to bring an outsider into the space. According to Zarah, only Orgun had ventured in and out of it. What would happen to the enchanted room if the dungeon died? Would all that knowledge be lost forever?

"I'm sorry, but we must continue," I said.

"Already? It's only been fifteen minutes! I thought we might even nap a bit," Carine said.

I pointed in the direction we'd been heading before. "We will sleep when we have no other option. Perhaps once we reach the next level, we'll reward ourselves with sleep."

Five minutes after we left the rest area, Toxin appeared beside me and whispered, "There are creatures in the darkness.

They've taken notice of our group. Some of them are rather large. Use caution if you continue on this path." He disappeared before I could ask him for more information.

"Don't make any sudden movements, but we may have company soon," I said as we continued.

"What do you —" Carine began to ask, but Helatha hissed.

"Silence, fool. We are being watched."

"Ew!" Carine said as she paused and looked down at her foot. It was coated in a thick slime. Moving her torch to the ground, she traced the line of thick mucus into the darkness.

A whistling sound alerted us to the first projectile. The small dart bounced from Xagrim with a *plink*. Dozens more followed from varying directions. I summoned a wall of force that protected one side while raising my shield to protect from the direction facing away from Xagrim. The onslaught continued for minutes, pausing only periodically. Many of them missed us completely, as if the attackers were extremely bad at ranged combat.

"Are we simply going to grovel here and wait to be filled with darts?" Helatha asked as she ducked a dart that bounced from my shield.

"No. We are waiting," I answered. Over the next few minutes, the rain of projectiles slowly died off.

"Are they leaving?" Carine asked from behind Xagrim's massive leg.

"In a manner of speaking," I said.

Moments later, Toxin appeared and tossed a small body to the ground.

"A psuthal. Just as we suspected. How many of them were there?" I asked.

"Two dozen killed. Three ran off into the caves. This is one I brought back for examination," Toxin answered flatly as he tossed a small body to the ground.

Kneeling, I inspected the creature. It was identical to the one I encountered the first time I entered the dungeon. A single stalked eye, worm-like teeth, gray skin with an elongated skull. It was roughly the size of an eight-year-old child. However, this one also wore a mesh armor and wielded a blowgun that appeared to be made of hollow bone. Touching the mesh armor, I found it slightly sticky. Using my dagger, I prodded it several times, testing its resistance. To my surprise, it was on par with cured leather, despite being as thick and flexible as sack cloth. I picked up several of the darts to inspect them.

Toxin likewise picked up one of the projectiles littered around us and sniffed it before touching the tip to his tongue. "Deathspore poison. One dart would not be lethal, but three or four would result in death in thirty to sixty minutes, depending on body composition and size. Paralysis and weakness would precede death."

"Can you synthesize an antivenom?"

"Perhaps, but it would take time."

"Have spells for poison," Gogbog offered.

"Keep them at the ready, just in case, old shaman. If no one is injured, we'll continue on," I said.

"Continue on? I need my heart to stop fluttering like a zippermouse," Carine said.

"Any idea how much farther?" I asked as I checked each group member over for stray darts that could be lodged in their armor or clothing.

Carine waved her sensor back and forth. "Judging by the fluctuations, maybe another mile."

"Good. Perhaps we will make it to the next level soon. I'd like to make it through two levels before we rest."

"Two?" Carine said incredulously.

Toxin suddenly stiffened before stepping backward into the shadows. "Something comes."

"Be prepared, everyone. Take up positions behind this rock formation!" I said as we moved toward the cover. A rumbling began to shake the ground.

"Must be thousands of 'em!" Carine said as she glanced around nervously.

The vibrations and noise grew louder, but I couldn't make out the direction. Were we being surrounded?

Dirt and rock bits exploded as something erupted from the ground nearby. Towering mammoth worms loomed above us, the tendrils along their blood-red bodies swaying as if searching for something to grab. These worms looked as if they could swallow a man whole. There were three of the large beasts, undulating back and forth as if waiting for one of us to move. Perhaps they hunted by vibration or sound.

Xagrim unsheathed his sword and took one step forward. The worm closest to him swerved with uncanny speed and bore down on the knight, its vast maw spread open for its next meal. Gogbog tumbled free of his harness just as the death knight disappeared completely down the worm's gullet. The knight's sword tumbled to the ground. For a moment, the faint outline of his form could be seen bulging in the worm's body as he was moved down its digestive tract.

"I think we're in trouble," Carina said.

CHAPTER TWELVE
Worm King

C arine looked as if she were about to have a nervous break-down. "We just lost Xagrim in one bite..."

"Yet they haven't attacked us," I replied. "Make no hostile movements."

Dozens of psuthals poured out of the darkness, armed with spears and blowguns. Surrounding us, they hissed and clicked, but did not attack.

"Put your hands up and do not resist," I said. It seemed they wanted to take us alive. While we might be able to win the fight even without Xagrim, there was no doubt most—if not all—of us would be poisoned in the process.

"We're just gonna to surrender without a fight?" Carine asked as the psuthals relieved her of her gear.

"For now," I said as I handed over my sword, shield, and bags. Once we were deprived of our weapons, the gathered psuthals became less agitated and hostile. Prodding us with the butts of their spears, they motioned for us to move in the direction we'd initially been traveling. "See? Not only are we heading toward the key, but we now have a guide."

Carine frowned but remained silent.

As we moved on through the dank, cool caverns, I began to notice what seemed like pathways or roads crossing through the areas we traveled. Stones and stalagmites had been cut away to make travel easier. Soon, we arrived at a rudimentary village that reminded me a bit of the goblin settlement connected to the dungeon. Dingy tents dotted the area, while glowing rocks gave off a dim light. I wondered if the rocks had been brought for our benefit, as psuthals had excellent vision in the dark.

There were no fires or smells of food cooking, as psuthals used their squirming teeth to sink into the flesh of their victims to draw out their vital fluids and nutrients. Rumors stated they could penetrate even light armor using this method of feeding.

We were led to the center of the village, where a vast mound of bones and skulls rose fifteen feet into the air. At the top, a large psuthal sat upon a throne. Its vibrant blue skin and glowing single eye wasn't the only thing that differentiated it from its brethren.

"Ssso we have visssitorss," it slurred through its rubbery teeth. "Ssso long sssince we lassst had visssitorsss. Who are you?"

"I am Jagen Therion, King of Tharune and master of the dungeon levels above. We need to travel below," I said with authority. Perhaps this minor subterranean chief could be cowed into submissiveness if I presented a strong front.

"Master? Legend ssays we usssed to have a master..." the unusual psuthal said.

The crowd murmured at his statement. Perhaps my title would be enough to see us through this.

"But he abandoned usss!" he said as he stood and shook a golden trident at the levels above. The crowd shouted and jeered as they also shook their weapons in frustration.

"Ancestors ssspeak of Massster, but I don't believe in him. Left us to rot, if he existed!" the tribal leader shouted. The crowd was becoming more agitated. If he whipped them into a fury, I had no doubt they would tear us to pieces.

"Imprisoned, no way out. Can't go up, can't go down. Mussst hunt for food, but we grow ssstrong! Overcome thingsss in darkness and rule!" the leader shouted. The crowd cheered. "Why do we need Master? Deep Onesss need no one...only UniPsu!" he shouted as he banged his fist against his chest.

When the cheering died down, he pointed to Carine. "How did you come down here? Where did you come from?"

"Umm...we came from the level above, down some steps."

"You lie! There is nothing above! No way out!" UniPsu shouted. "Only way out is through cracks and cavesss."

"We opened the door leading down. We did not know you were here. But now I need your help to go deeper into the dungeon," I said.

"Down? Can't go down! Bad things down. No way up! We try, but passage is sssealed! You lie! But...never seen people before. Had to come from somewhere..." UniPsu said as he paused to think.

"As I said, I now rule the dungeon above, and I've come down to...help your people again. I've disposed of the old Master and wish to once again open the dungeon to the psuthals," I said.

"Help? Open? How can you help? UniPsu is leader of Deep Ones, not Master!"

"You would retain your leadership. I have goblin tribes and others who follow me. In exchange, we can provide food, medicine, and wealth."

"Pfah! What do we need with human wealth! The ancient ssscripts say humans come into cavern to kill us and take our holy relics. Even if true that you came from above, better to close door and kill you," UniPsu said as he motioned toward his followers.

A whistle from the darkness caused them to hesitate. I held up my arm and made a fist. Toxin was signaling he was about to assassinate UniPsu, but my signal ordered him to pause.

"Stop!" I said as I unleashed my willpower across the cavern.

The gathered psuthal grew silent and looked about nervously as UniPsu stood from his throne. "What wasss that? What did you do?" the abnormal psuthal asked as his single eye stared intently at me.

"As I said, I am the leader of this dungeon. That was but a taste of my power. I could have killed you just now, but I wish for you to live. I see you are a great leader, and it would harm your people if you were dead."

UniPsu sat again and looked about nervously. "If...if Master has truly returned, then Deep Ones would prosper. But...how to determine if you are Massster and not a trick? Humansss are tricky..."

"You felt the power of my will; was that not enough?" I asked. It seemed that while my willpower was enough to bowl over or control minions above, the ones on this level merely felt it as a slight push, perhaps because they had been removed from the dungeon for so long.

"No. Not enough. Must show strength. Master is strong. Must prove to be strong. UniPsu wants to believe, but over-worlders lie. Bring Strong One. He is champion. If you defeat him, you prove that you are the Master and may go below."

Helatha chuckled. "You should have no problem overcoming whatever serves as a champion for these weak simpletons, Master."

I wondered what differentiated the Strong One from the others. While UniPsu appeared to be twice as large as the rest of the tribe, even he would probably present little challenge to me in combat.

The crowd parted, creating a path. Our group followed through the open space until we reached a large stone dome. Ledges wound around the dome, with small holes drilled into the surface. It reminded me of a giant colander. The gathered psuthals scrambled up the sides and stood upon the ledges, jamming their eye stalks into the holes.

"I don't like the look of this," Carine said.

The king arrived on the back of one of the giant worms, which lifted him to the very top of the dome where a seat awaited. He leaned forward and put his eye into the drilled hole.

"Enter, supposed Master, and face the Ssstrong One," he shouted.

My party walked with me to the entrance. Peering in, it was too dark to see what I was to face.

"Do not fear, master. I will cast hexes upon your foe so as to weaken him if necessary," Helatha offered.

"I've my own spells. I'm sure I'll make short work of this champion," I said. "Don't do anything unless something goes wrong. We don't want to anger them."

"As you wish."

Upon stepping into the dome, I noticed the floor had been smoothed out and flattened. It took a minute for my eyes to adjust to the lower light levels, but at least a small amount trickled in through the few open holes in the structure.

Across the arena, I now noticed a figure. Its single stalked eye swiveled about until it rested on me. While it looked slightly taller than a regular psuthal, I expected it would present no problem in combat. Then it stood up.

Now I could see it was a foot taller than I was and much more muscular. It hissed as it took a step forward.

"You can take him!" Carine shouted from the side.

"Slay him for Castigous, Master!" Helatha said.

I wondered if my opponent was armed. If so, my armor would be a boon, but if not, it would be a hindrance. I circled the edge of the arena as I tried to make out more details about my opponent. While UniPsu hadn't mentioned a ban on magic, I wondered what his reaction would be upon seeing it used. It would definitely be proof of my power and strength. Perhaps several blinding orbs of light to stun my opponent, followed up by a fireball to finish him quickly. Such a spectacle would cause fear and chaos among the primitive psuthals watching, while also keeping me out of harm's way.

"Multae Illuminous Manifestae!" I shouted. A small spark flew from my fingertip and fizzled out. I looked down at my hands in confusion. "Illuminous Manifestae!" I shouted. Nothing happened.

"Master, look at the sigils!" Helatha shouted. Looking around, I now saw the faint outline of archaic sigils beginning to glow faintly on the walls. The area within the dome must have contained an anti-magic field.

"Just great," I said as I moved away from the Strong One. That also meant Helatha wouldn't be able to assist from outside with her spells.

My towering opponent suddenly rushed toward me, leaping into the air and spinning once he was a dozen feet away. *Crack! Crack!* I stumbled backward as something struck my breastplate with tremendous force. Was he throwing rocks? I backpedaled as he watched me retreat, obviously confused that his attack hadn't disabled me.

"Kill him, Strong One!" UniPsu shouted from high above. The leader's command awoke the behemoth from his confused stupor. Again, he rushed forward and jerked. Something slapped the side of my arm, just missing the plate armor, but stinging like a red-hot iron even through the leather and padding. It felt like a whip. Looking back, I noticed the large psuthal's gait was rather unusual...as if it didn't have arms to swing to balance it. Again, it jerked one side of its body and something whistled by my helmet, striking the wall behind me. This psuthal possessed deadly natural weapons that the others did not.

Slowing a bit, I danced to the side as the monster jerked again. It held the advantage at medium range. I'd have to find a way to engage it close — but could my fists do any damage to the rubbery, muscled creature?

I worked my way closer, inch by inch, dodging as my opponent rhythmically lashed back and forth, building up speed until I was under assault by a flurry of attacks. Wherever it struck my less armored areas, it felt as if a fire had been ignited against my flesh. I would end up black and blue for days at this rate — if I survived. I thought of Zarah and the dungeon.

I covered my face with my arms and dashed in, allowing several of the lashes to land against me as I barreled into the confused monster. In close range, it would no longer be able to use its long appendages as weapons.

Before I could act, both of its long arms slithered around my body like twin snakes, holding me fast. Each time I moved, they tightened slightly. I may have made a grave miscalculation.

"It is over!" UniPsu shouted victoriously from above. The crowd cheered.

"Don't give up!" Carine shouted.

Flexing my muscles against the creature, its grip loosened slightly. Its face seemed to indicate a moment of surprise that I could challenge its physical strength. Yet my forceful exertions were limited by my stamina, while its arms seemed to never tire. After a moment I relaxed my struggle, allowing it to grip me tighter. My breaths shortened as I gasped against its powerful appendages. Each time that I fought back, the leathery arms constricted slightly tighter. This was the same method large snakes in jungle regions used to kill their prey.

With a screech, it opened its mouth wide and lowered it upon my shoulder and neck. The wriggling teeth squirmed and searched as they invaded the spaces in my armor, several of them finding open flesh to burrow into. Stars began to dance across my vision as I became lightheaded due to the immediate blood loss.

"No...I'm not finished yet," I whispered as I finally maneuvered my hand and arm into position. I hadn't been blindly attempting to break its grip but to retrieve one of the poison darts I'd pocketed earlier. With several quick jabs, I felt the weapon pierce the blubbery skin of my opponent a half dozen times. It continued to feed, but after a moment its grip loosened just enough to get my arm free. Twisting about, I jammed the poisoned dart into the thing's mouth until it released me. It backed away, its tentacled arms lashing wildly in pain.

Rushing forward, I kicked the monster, sending it flailing against a nearby wall. Again, and again I punched its midsection and face, my armored fists acting like makeshift battering rams. It fell to its knees, stunned senseless. Bringing both hands up, I brought them down on its misshapen skull, causing the Strong One to collapse against the hard ground. It did not move again. I wasn't sure if it was dead or unconscious, but I was too exhausted to care. Either way, the fight was finished.

The crowd that had cheered earlier fell silent. Many began jeering and hissing.

Despite my exhaustion, I once again released my will against them. "Silence!" Walking to the door, I banged on it three times. It opened. "Illuminous Manifestae!" I shouted once outside. A blinding orb of light much brighter than the ones I'd summoned earlier erupted and dazzled the gathered psuthal, who were making their way down from their ledges. Several fell to the ground, unable to see.

"I've completed your task. Provide me with the key immediately and show me to the doorway to the next level," I boomed.

"No! No! You...you cheated! Ssstrong One is not defeated!" UniPsu shouted as he leapt upon the back of a giant worm and stamped up and down. "Kill him, worm! Eat him up!" The giant worm upon which the tribe's leader was perched opened its gaping maw and reared back.

"Xagrim," I said as I sent out a mental command.

The giant worm paused and shuddered before jerking from side to side. It hissed and spasmed as UniPsu held on for dear life. The giant worm's body turned to an ashen gray color as it ceased moving and froze completely. Xagrim strode forth from its belly as the beast's flesh turned to dust. The entire creature collapsed upon its own weight, forming a messy pile of dust particles on which the leader of the psuthals fell. Coughing and hacking, he rolled out of the remains and wiped his single eye as he blinked in confusion.

Xagrim, Helatha, and I stared down upon him as I held out my hand. "Give me the key. Now."

CHAPTER THIRTEEN
Honor and Duty

The psuthal led us away from their village and down a well-worn path that ended with a metal door embedded into the cavern wall. Upon seeing me pull out the key, the group of diminutive warriors retreated in fear.

"It seems there's something they fear down below. What will we face?" Helatha asked.

"The staff stated it would most likely be undead of some type," I said as I ran my hands across the door. The protective magic was much weaker than on the door above in the throne room. Given sufficient power, a single high-level magic user or group could potentially break through given enough time. If we succeeded, I would need to find a way to strengthen the enchantments or else forgo forcing a group to get the key in the first place. The key slid in and turned easily.

"Excellent. My control of the undead will make our journey much easier. Perhaps I'll pick up one or two minions to add to our ranks as souvenirs," the soul snatcher bragged.

"Let's see what we face first before making predictions," I said as Xagrim and I made our way down the steps. Toxin disappeared into the darkness, presumably to scout ahead. The winding stairwell seemed to go on forever. Was this level that much deeper than the others, or was it my imagination? On the last few steps, I stumbled as sweat poured into my eyes.

"Master! What's wrong?" Helatha asked as she rushed to my side. Helatha and Xagrim helped me down to the floor, propping me up against the wall. A moment later, Toxin reappeared, ready for combat.

"Get his armor off, fools!" Helatha ordered as she looked me over. With the help of Carine and Toxin, they were able to remove my breastplate and the underlying layers of leather and padded armor.

"These wounds on your neck and shoulder need treatment. The flow of blood continues," Helatha said as she retrieved bandages from her bag.

"A-anticoagulant," I said as I began to shiver. I'd thought the wetness I'd felt running down my chest and back had been sweat, but I'd forgotten the psuthal's strange teeth also injected a chemical to stem the coagulation of the blood of their victims.

"By Castigous...you're covered in bruises and welts in addition to the puncture wounds! My healing abilities require some...sacrifice. Who will give up their life force for the Master?" Helatha asked.

Toxin stepped forward. "Take mine."

The soul snatcher shook her head. "No, you are something between life and death. It must be the shaman or the gnome. I cannot cast this dark healing upon myself." She stared at Carine.

"I...well, don't I need my life force to...live?" Carine said meekly.

"Fool, I do not care —" Helatha said before being interrupted by Gogbog, who slowly moved passed her, using his staff as a walking stick. Stamping his staff to the ground, he muttered a few indecipherable words. Two small totems appeared, pulsing with green light. The waves of healing magic washed over me, alleviating my symptoms.

"Be fine, soon," the elder shaman said as he walked away and eased himself to the floor, where he pulled out a long bone pipe and began puffing.

"See? Be fine, soon," Carine said as she moved as far away from Helatha as the room would allow.

"Should we make camp, Master? You should rest after your battle," Helatha asked.

"No...we have to keep moving. We'll only rest when the entire group requires it. Once these healing totems are finished, I will be fine."

After a small meal, we gathered our things.

Toxin spoke from the shadows. "The immediate area is clear of creatures. I disabled a few ancient traps. If I find more, I will deal with them."

"Good job," I said as Xagrim and I moved through the door. This level resembled the first level of the dungeon above. Stone floors and walls that looked to be part of a castle or other man-made structure. Each room was either a storage room or barracks.

"I don't understand this place...why would this level be so different from the last one?" Carine asked. "I've seen it in other places of power and dungeons. Like someone took bits and pieces and shuffled them on a whim. You never know what to expect as you move through them."

"Yisan said a powerful dungeon lord can move levels around as it suits his desires or even create them from his mind. I don't know why Orgun rearranged them as he did," I explained. "Perhaps it had to do with magic requirements or strategic defense. Maybe he moved the levels that required too much magic to maintain to the bottom then closed them off as the dungeon fell into disrepair."

"You are probably correct," Helatha said as she bandaged the nearly healed wound on my neck then helped me into my armor.

We continued to explore the level, but it seemed completely abandoned. Layers of dust and ancient spider webs covered every surface. Not even skeletons remained of the previous occupants. Why were the psuthals so terrified of this floor? It appeared to be empty.

"Can you detect the key?" I asked Carine.

She checked her readings then spun about slowly. Tapping the glass of the sensor several times, she shrugged. "It's here, but it keeps moving. Like...through the walls or something."

"Then there's obviously something here with us. Be wary," I said.

We continued down the hallways Carine indicated we should use but came to dead ends time and again. After thirty minutes, it was apparent some entity was keeping the key from us.

"Should we split up and try to surround them?" Carine asked.

"Without knowing more about our opponent or opponents, that could prove risky," I answered.

"Spirits. Angry spirits," Gogbog said.

"Spirits? As in ghosts?" Carine asked.

Helatha closed her eyes and muttered a dark prayer. "The goblin is correct. There are supernatural entities around us, but they are keeping their distance. Perhaps they fear my power."

"Or maybe they're just toying with us," I said. "Is there anything you can do to draw them out?"

"Perhaps. It would be easier to block them in, however. Come this way," Helatha said as she led the group back down the hall where we'd just traveled. Upon reaching the end, she pulled a vial of blood from her satchel and began scrawling sigils upon the walls, floors, and ceilings. "They won't be able to pass through these."

We backtracked through another hallway, and she repeated the procedure until there was only one hall left to venture down.

Carine checked her machine. "Looks like they are bouncing back and forth and are confused."

"Then we have them cornered," I said as I took the lead.

"Wait. Only certain spells will harm spirits. Allow me to place a spell of necrotic energy upon your blade, Master," Helatha said. "While it possesses durability enchantments, it will do nothing against beings from the beyond."

"What about my weapons and the big guy?" Carine asked.

"I've already sapped much of my magic covering such large areas with binding spells. I won't waste what little I have left," Helatha said with disdain. She drew close and ran her hand along my sword. It began crackling with black bolts of energy.

Smiling, she leaned in close and whispered, "Let me know if you need anything else, Master."

"Thank you, Helatha," I said as I pulled away from her cold touch. "Xagrim, lead the way."

After a short walk, the end of the long hall came into view, yet it was empty. Had the spirits slipped through our defenses?

"Are you sure your gadget is functioning properly?" I whispered to Carine.

The gnome shook the Key Zoomer several times. "As far as I can tell. Whatever it is remains right there."

"Enough timidity," Xagrim said as he removed Gogbog from his harness and stomped down the hall. Out of midair, he ripped an armored spectral warrior and slammed it against the wall. Its ghostly green blade scraped against Xagrim's armor, eliciting a rain of green sparks. The hulking death knight drove it against the wall again, then reversed direction, jerking his opponent into the opposite wall.

Xagrim was then lifted from his feet and was tossed down the hallway by an unseen force, sliding several feet until he came to a rest in front of us. "Cowards," he said as icy breath swirled from the darkness of his helm.

"Cowards? We who fought for the king until death, and who fight for him in death? What do you know of heroism, false knight?" a decrepit voice said from somewhere ahead of us. A picture flew from the wall and smashed to the ground as a tapestry was torn to shreds.

"I think you made them mad," Carine said.

"Our fury knows no bounds. Our lust for vengeance is supreme. Who dare invades our sanctuary?" the voice called out.

"I am King Jagen Therion, ruler of Tharune and this dungeon. I seek the key to the next floor. I know you possess it," I called out to the formless entities.

"King...of Tharune? Master? Have you finally returned to us after all this time? We have waited so long..." the hollow voice said as it drew closer. "But...wait! No! You are not the king! You bear some semblance, but you are far too young! You lie, invader! We must protect the key, men!" the voice shouted as it drew farther away.

A group of five spectral armored knights faded into view, armed with longswords, shields, maces, and war hammers. "We've been charged with protecting the key from all interlopers. We shall not fail our sacred duties!" the knight with the most ornate armor said.

"Wait...those tabards...those have the crest of my family upon them," I said.

"It seems they once served the King of Old Vadis, your ancestor," Helatha said.

"If only I had the royal seal with me, perhaps this fight could be avoided," I said as I raised my shield to defend. "At least they will be hampered by the closed-in hallway, giving us an advantage."

"Be careful, Master. Fighting spirits is not like fighting mortal men," Helatha warned as she pulled the Aeon Torment, Castigous' bible, from her bag.

One of the ghostly warrior's mace came down in a smashing arc. Raising my shield, I was shocked to feel part of the weapon impact my arm. It was as if the shield had provided only partial protection.

"Use your sword, Master!" Helatha said.

For his next blow, I turned away his mace with my now-ensorcelled blade, which blocked it completely. Unfortunately, it left my hand numb from the powerful spirit's unearthly strength.

Xagrim's blade erupted in a blue flame. His massive two-handed weapon slammed into the ghostly knights' weapons repeatedly, leaving swirls of green and blue magic as the weapons came away from each other. Despite the death knight's tremendous power, the duo of knights seemed to be his equal.

The knights in the back suddenly leapt through their compatriots, bringing their weapons down upon us. It was then I noticed their weapons were passing through the walls, floor, and ceiling until they solidified right before striking us. It seemed we were the only ones hampered by the tight hall. We were slowly being driven back by the combination attacks of the ghostly knights.

Black sparkling magic rained down upon them like a decaying mushroom's spores. The knights coughed and groaned.

"I've placed a hex of weakness upon them; it will only last moments," Helatha said.

"Follow my lead!" I shouted as we slowly moved backward down the hall until we encountered one of the large barracks. We needed room to fight more than our opponents did.

"Sure wish I had some weapons that could do something," Carine complained. "Wait, weren't there five of them?"

Helatha screamed as a knight rose through the floor behind us, his blade tearing through her cloak and slicing open her back. He drew his blade back for the finishing blow, but Toxin's twin blades sank into his armor to the hilts. Whirling about, his armored fist found nothing as the rogue disappeared into the shadows.

"Craven coward!" the knight shouted at the fleeing rogue.

Helatha tried to reach around to the wound on her back but collapsed to the floor in agony.

"I help," Gogbog said as he summoned a totem of healing. Whirling his staff, he recited another incantation, which summoned a blue spectral bear. The beast's roar shook the dust from the ceiling as the shaman pointed toward the knight behind us. "Stop bad spirit," the shaman instructed.

"Everyone is helping but me!" Carine complained. "Look out, Jagen! To your left, Xagrim! Use your sword! Get that guy, scary rogue man!"

"That...is not helping," I said as I dodged a massive war hammer that completely smashed in the side of a decaying dresser. A sword erupted through the middle of the knight who had just swung at me as his fellow knight dove through his compatriot. Jerking to the side, the blade partially pierced my breastplate, slicing open the flesh under a rib. These tactics where several of them could attack at once while ignoring their compatriots were almost impossible to compensate for.

"Your king is a coward! Your kingdom is full of blackguards and infidels! King Therion is an idiot!" Carine shouted.

"How dare you insult the king?" one of the knights said as he turned toward the gnome. Xagrim's sword caught him directly in the midsection, leaving a deep gash in his armor as the ghost knight sailed across the room and through a wall.

"*That*...actually might be helping," I said as I parried the lead knight's longsword.

"The Order of Tharune will not fall this day!" the powerful leader shouted as he redoubled his attacks. Sweat drenched my body and the wound on my side began to throb. I still hadn't fully recovered from the battle above. We were pushing ourselves too fast through the dungeon. I suddenly wished Zarah was present to serenade us with her strength and vitality songs. We were holding our own, but these knights didn't tire like we were. Xagrim and Toxin wouldn't be able to protect Carine, Helatha, and Gogbog against five foes if we grew too exhausted.

"What...is...happening?" the knight behind us shouted. I cast a glance over to find the edges of his form were beginning to trail away like smoke. It looked like Toxin's Susperon-B worked even on these strong spirits. With one mighty swipe, the goblin shaman's spirit bear tore through the knight's sword and helm, smearing the knight out of existence like oil paints on an artist's palette. The knight's scream faded away into nothing. The bear fell from its standing position and sniffed the air, apparently guarding the three rear members from further attack.

"Foul miscreants, what have you done to Sir Darion?" the leader shouted as he struck hard against my sword. It felt as if Helatha's hex may be fading. We needed to finish this quickly. It was hard to maneuver the remaining knights to give Toxin an opening, due to the fact they were not hamstrung by physical barriers. One in front could easily slash through his comrade behind him in order to strike out at Toxin, while the one in the back's blade struck at us. It was a totally alien style of combat compared to how we normally fought.

"Can't you use your...shout or whatever it was to convince them you're the king?" Carine said as she held a bloody compress to Helatha's gaping wound.

"No..." I said as I struck hard against a ghost knight's shield, leaving a deep gouge in the translucent metal. "I've used it too much, too quickly."

"I told you we needed to rest," she chided.

"Now is not the time, Carine," I said as I jumped back from a war hammer strike.

"Hollow woman safe, help now," Gogbog said as he struggled to rise with the assistance of his staff. After a short incantation, a small gray totem appeared slightly ahead of our group. Upon its first pulse, the knights began to move slower.

"Egad! What is happening? It's as if my armor has doubled in weight!" the leader shouted. My next blow cleaved his pauldron and penetrated the metal so deeply that it should have pierced his shoulder. Before he could react, the knight behind him clobbered him in the helm with his war hammer.

"Sir Horild, what..." he said as he began to turn.

"I-I know not what is happening, Sir Pomeron! It's as if my body has been magicked!" the larger knight with the hammer explained.

"It is the witch! Kill the —" Sir Pomeron shouted before my sword slid through his neck. His eyes bulged before he fell to the floor and faded away. The key remained where his body had fallen. Glowing blue, the key seemed to be as spectral as the knights themselves. Hopefully it would prove to be more tangible.

"Save the key!" the knight beside him shouted as he dove for it. Toxin's dagger slashed across the back of his knee, causing the knight to trip before he could reach it. Purgatory removed the knight's head from his shoulders before he could rise again. With the odds in our favor, we pushed the remaining knight back with the assistance of his companion, who had now apparently switched sides. I glanced back at Helatha, who held an outstretched hand toward Sir Horild as if she were grasping his very soul. Her forehead was slick with sweat as she grimaced in pain.

"I...can't hold him...much longer..." she said as she strained against her spell or dark prayer.

"Lead him to me," I said as Toxin, Xagrim, and Sir Horild ganged up upon the last opposing knight.

Xagrim and Horild battered the flailing knight with their massive weapons as Toxin darted in and struck him in the arm between the joints of his armor. Unable to hold his weapon any longer, his spectral sword fell to the ground and sank into the stone.

"Tharune shall not fall, miscreants," the knight said as I brought my sword down upon his neck, relieving him of his ghostly head. Just as Sir Horild broke free of Helatha's control, I ran him through before he could act. Perhaps not the most honorable way to be vanquished, but I was too exhausted to care.

"That...was...amazing!" Carine said as the ghostly forms sank into the ground. "You've managed to kill ghosts! How does that work, anyhow?"

I paused for a second to catch my breath. "They...are not dead. Given time, they will reform on their own, even without any help from the dungeon. How long do you think we have, Helatha?"

The soul snatcher looked as if she were about to faint. Her wound and exertions had taken a lot out of her. "I...believe it will most likely take...several days. You inflicted severe damage to their forms, and the flow of magic in the dungeon is almost nonexistent."

"Good. We have the key, but we will need time to heal our injuries and recover our magical reserves. We'll set up camp here." Pausing, I thought of the knights we'd just defeated. They were not evil or corrupted, but merely convinced they were protecting Vadis from invaders. They seemed to suffer under the delusion that they still lived, and Vadis stood. As their current king, I couldn't help but feel a twinge of guilt at our victory. Yet, as the dungeon's master, it was encouraging to realize these knights would become powerful minions if we succeeded.

"Prepare for camp but remain on guard."

CHAPTER FOURTEEN
Short Respite

Our injuries and depleted magic required at least a full night's rest to remedy. The dangers would most likely grow stronger the deeper we went and forging ahead while exhausted meant certain doom.

Retrieving thick blankets and padding from our bags, Carine, Helatha, and I set up our sleeping areas. I assisted the elderly shaman with his bedding. He grunted and groaned as he lowered himself to the ground, his ancient joints popping and creaking. I'd been surprised by his usefulness during the battle. Despite his age, he'd contributed tremendously to our success. The ancient nature magic he wielded was powerful indeed.

After tending to Gogbog, I checked Xagrim over. The knight had been devoured alive and the knights had proved to be strong fighters. Areas of slight corrosion dotted the death knight's metal body, along with a few deep gashes and several new dents. He seemed unaffected by all of it. Of course, his armored form was not a suit of armor, but rather his actual true form. Healing spells worked on him just as they did any liv-

139

ing being. A night of convalescence would remedy most of the damage. If something happened to him or Toxin, I wasn't sure we could spare the magic from our portable sphere to bring them back, and with the Soul Sphere leaking magic, they could be lost forever.

After a quick meal of bread, dried fruit, and meat, we settled in, stowing the rest of our gear and armor and dressing our wounds. After spending so many months sleeping in my plush bed alone, sharing a room with this motley crew felt awkward. I was used to jimps, goblins, and gloobs taking care of my every need. This would be a good experience for me. Despite my daily training, I was worried about becoming soft as I spent most of my time settling petty disputes between guild members or attempting to quell riots and protests through Leath or the others. Spending a few days in the field in a combat situation was just what I needed to regain my edge.

Gogbog summoned one last totem of healing before he surrendered to sleep for the night. Its soothing healing properties washed over the entire group as we relaxed. Each pulse was akin to a fractional healing spell that slowly knit flesh back together a few cells at a time and caused broken bones to reset in their normal positions and begin to grow together. While not as powerful or fast as a cleric's healing spell, it had the benefit of affecting the whole party and being more efficient.

Toxin sat with his back against the wall, checking over his weapons and vials of poison. Xagrim stood resolute in the doorway, ready to intercept any enemy that appeared during our rest.

"How is your wound, Helatha?" I asked as I knelt beside the injured soul snatcher.

"It is nothing. I apologize for succumbing to such a clumsy attack," she answered.

"Your domination spell helped turn the tide of battle and ended the conflict early. You performed admirably, even with such a grievous wound," I said.

She smiled. "I do what I must to assist you, Master. I would gladly give my own life if it means your success."

Her devotion was...unnerving. While Toxin and Xagrim did my bidding without question, they also seemed to be less than human, as if their spirits were enslaved. While Helatha was also a minion, she was a spirit who lived in the stolen form of a human. She wasn't bound by the Penance of Fate like some of the others, yet her loyalty was just as strong. I wanted to know more about her, yet I was concerned any questioning would be mistaken as romantic interest and lead to encouraging her amorous affections. While she still probed for my interest from time to time, it seemed she'd given up for now. Perhaps at a future date I'd ask more of her history.

I returned to my own bedding, pulled out a sharpening stone, and worked it along Purgatory's length. Even with the recent enchantments to make it more durable, when dealing with supernatural and magical creatures, regular maintenance was necessary. Several times I looked down the length of the blade to catch Carine watching me. "Do you have something you wish to ask me?" I finally asked after the third time.

"I can't believe I'm exploring a dungeon with the King of Tharune! It's so exciting! Thank you for inviting me! Everyone in the guild was so jealous! I can't believe how lucky I am!" she gushed.

"You do realize you could die here, correct?" I asked.

"Of course I do! That's what makes it so exciting! Danger, mystery, and magic around every corner! Monsters! Treasure...well, we haven't found any treasure so far, but imagine when we do! Epic battles shared with loyal allies! It's...it's just too much!" the feisty gnome replied.

Helatha looked as if she wanted to ask me what I was thinking in bringing the young gnome. Toxin showed me one of his daggers and raised an eyebrow, as if saying, "Just say the word."

"After reading Kurth's report about you and your guild, I was...impressed. Your mechanical knowledge is rather astounding. I hear a few of your inventions were even put on display at the Royal Magic Academy," I said.

"I just see a problem, and I try and figure out how to solve it. It bugs the fire out of me if there's something I can't figure out," Carine said. "I know! I could show you all of my inventions! I've brought about a dozen of them along! Just let me get my bag!"

"No! I mean...no, thank you. I'm very tired after those battles and wish to relax for a period. Time is of the essence if we are going to save the dungeon."

"I understand completely! I didn't have a chance to help out much with the battles, but if that UniPsu had tried anything, I was ready to let him have it with my Armapult 500!" she said as she rolled over to grab a strange device she'd worn on her arm earlier. I'd meant to ask about it but didn't want to set her off on another dissertation.

"I'm looking forward to witnessing it in action. It looks...formidable," I replied as I rolled over and doused the last remaining orb of light. Several candles caused shadows to dance across the walls and ceiling.

"What's it like being a king and dungeon master?" Carine asked after a moment of silence.

I sighed. Without turning to face her, I looked up at the ceiling as I replied, "Tiresome. I have more responsibilities than you can imagine."

"It's probably pretty nice being able to do whatever you want and having all that wealth, though, right?"

"No. I can do nothing and go nowhere. My wealth is merely a means to an end. I would trade it all for my old freedom again," I said as a vision of Aiyla flashed into my mind. The pain of her loss stung just as much now as it did then.

Carine rolled over on her stomach and propped her head up with her hands. "Really? I had...no idea. That's not how I imagined it would be for someone as powerful as you."

I chuckled. "Powerful? I feel powerless almost every day. Powerless to save the city that is crumbling. Powerless to protect my dungeon. Powerless to find my missing family. Powerless to change a world that needs changing. But enough of such matters. Tell me a bit about yourself, Carine." With the gnome's tendency to ramble on, I hoped I wasn't making a mistake by asking, but despite my exhaustion, I found myself wide awake. Perhaps her conversation would help me drift off.

"Oh, you know — my father was a tinker, so I picked that up at an early age. Always trying to make something from the junk around the house. We lived pretty well, as we could fix just about anything someone brought to us. Our little cottage turned into what some might call a junkyard over the years as we collected anything and everything. I studied engineering for a while but found books and tests to be boring. The real knowledge was out in the field...so I started volunteering on some low-level quests until I worked my way into some of the guilds, and we went down into the *really* interesting places."

"Such as?" I asked.

"Hmm, well, one place I enjoyed was the old mines just up from Ironpit. We'd heard some rumors of creatures living out of there. Turned out to be a den of all manner of beasties. The deeper we went, the more apparent it became the place was under the control of something. I found a lot of old dwarven tools and inventions that I hadn't seen before. It was all over once we ran into a pair of obsidian golems, and we had to turn back. Never did find out what was running the place. Lost one group member on that quest," the gnome said as she stared off into the distance.

To my surprise, Helatha seemed to be listening to the gnome's tales with genuine interest. "So, you do this mainly to discover lost knowledge and technology, I take it?"

"The gold and gems don't hurt, but yeah, I want to find what there is in the world. Some of the old technology is even superior to what we use today. I've got a few patents based off of these devices that use steam to generate energy. I'm also working on a way to transmit energy through gold wire, but it's an expensive process."

"Power through wires...fascinating. I'd like to look at your notes sometime, if you don't mind," I said. "Perhaps the kingdom could fund some of your studies and inventions."

The gnome appeared speechless for a moment. "I'd...really appreciate that, Your Highness."

"Jagen is fine. No need for formalities while we battle for our lives deep in a dungeon."

"Master, I believe we should get some rest. It's getting late," Helatha said.

While Carine's conversation had been mentally stimulating, my body still felt as if it had been turned to lead. Every joint ached, and the bruises and cuts I'd accumulated still throbbed, despite the poultices and spells working to mend them as quickly as possible. I could sip on a healing potion to speed up the process slightly, but they were rare, and I didn't want to waste it just to ease my discomfort.

"You're right, of course. We've socialized too long," I said as I rolled over to face away from the group.

It seemed Carine had finally gotten the message, as she pulled out a notebook and began making notes. I found the scratching annoying at first, but it soon became comforting.

Casting an innocuous glance at Toxin, I was surprised to see his eyes closed, but even more shocked to see the third eye in the center of his forehead was now active. It swiveled about with inhuman speed, darting from person to person and focusing on each movement or sound. Toxin was sound asleep but was well-protected by the vigilant eye. I'd wondered about the purpose of it ever since he emerged from the Penance of Fate, and now I knew. It would be impossible to take the rogue unawares while he rested.

Despite my exhaustion, I found sleep to be elusive. A vision of the Soul Sphere slowly leaking the dungeon's lifeblood while Zarah's worried face loomed above it appeared in my thoughts. Was it my imagination caused by weariness, some sort of link to the dungeon we'd left above, or a premonition of what was to come? I wanted to call out to her, to allay her fears.

"Allow me to assist you, Master," Helatha whispered as she crawled closer. She placed her frigid hand on my shoulder.

"I've made myself clear, Helatha…" I said.

"No, I see you are disturbed. A simple sleep spell will guide you to slumber. A very minor cantrip," she said.

"Very well," I said reluctantly. Time was of the essence, and we all needed as much rest as possible. I couldn't let my fears and doubts prevent a good night's rest.

Helatha whispered her spell and stared down at me with amusement as my body relaxed and my eyes grew heavy. "Sleep well, Master," she cooed as she gently ran her fingers down my face and sealed my eyes for the night.

"AWAKEN," A GRIM VOICE ordered from the darkness.

In a sleepy haze, I asked, "What time is it?"

"Unknown and irrelevant. We must complete our mission, or we will all die," Xagrim said.

Looking around, everyone else in the group had already begun packing up the camp.

"We let you sleep in since you had the worst of it yesterday," Carine said cheerfully.

"I believe it is still early morn, Master," Helatha said. "We dare not rest for too long while the Soul Sphere grows weaker by the minute." After lecturing everyone else on the importance of time, I felt foolish for being the last to awaken.

After a quick breakfast of dried meat, nuts, and an apple, I stowed my gear and donned my armor again. We lifted Gogbog back into his harness on Xagrim's back and were then ready to depart for the next level.

The hall in which we'd battled the ghostly knights held the massive metal door leading down. The lock resisted the spectral key, which felt as if it might disappear from my hand. After several attempts, the lock turned. The enchantments on this door felt extremely weak. Given enough time, I was sure our party could probably break the door down, but it would drain some of our magic and strength, leaving us unable to continue until we'd rested for a full day or longer. I wondered if the enchantments on the next doors would be in the same state. It could prove problematic if the enchantments grew weaker. If we succeeded, we would need the doors at full strength to protect the new Soul Sphere.

Upon making the trek down the stairwell, Toxin left the landing room to scout the floor.

"What's going to be on this level?" Carine asked.

"The staff wasn't specific, but stated if we were smart, there should be no physical danger," I said. I didn't mention I'd felt like the animated staff was withholding something at the time as if it didn't want me to know what we would face. Perhaps I was just being paranoid.

After thirty minutes, Toxin still hadn't returned.

Carine peered around the edge of the door. "Do you think something happened to him? Perhaps he was eaten by a dragon! Or maybe transported to a different world...or —"

"We'll give him a few more minutes before looking for him. Perhaps he is lost," I said. I didn't really believe the exguild leader could get lost, and I was beginning to get worried, but I wouldn't let the other group members see my concern.

The minutes ticked by, each seemingly longer than the last. Carine used her device to search for the key, swiveling back and forth with a confused look.

"Problem?" I asked.

"Well...one minute the needle is here, then the signal jumps over here, then nothing, then it registers something over there. The signal is weak. Maybe something's interfering with it, like a strange magical source. I can't tell where the key is, or even if there is one."

"All right, we've waited long enough. Let's move out and find Toxin and the key," I said as Xagrim and I cautiously moved into the dark hall outside the room. I summoned an orb and sent it down the hall until it came to a stop in front of a solid black door. There were no other branches or doorways, simply a single path. It reminded me a bit of the level containing the Dire Hall. Would we face an enemy that surpassed our abilities like when Zarah and I had stumbled upon Xagrim guarding the throne room? Had Toxin met his fate against something that dwarfed his abilities?

"Stay back a bit," I said as I approached the door with my shield readied. Grasping the knob, I turned it slowly until the door released. A thin beam of light poured forth. I cautiously opened the door the rest of the way as a bright, chaotic light filled the dim hall, causing us to shield our eyes.

Once my eyes had adjusted, I gasped in despair at the horror we faced. "No...not this. Anything but this," I whispered.

CHAPTER FIFTEEN
Mental Anguish

C arine stepped into the room and screamed, "It looks...so fun!" she shouted as she jumped up and down.

"No, this is torture. Far more torturous than Ho'Scar's chamber," I argued.

Lights danced and flashed in front of us as various objects shifted in space across pathways that stood above gaping chasms that seemingly went on forever. It was as if someone had carved the floor out into puzzling paths and jigsaws that ended for no reason or doubled back in other directions with no purpose in mind. Each platform contained teleporters — dozens of teleporters. In addition to the flashing teleporters, each platform contained a raised pedestal with a plaque on it. Looking around, the teleporters seemed to be flashing because they contained small objects such as an insect, pebbles, or other trash that had accumulated over the years.

"I love puzzles!" Carine said as she rushed to the first display.

"Gods, save me," I said as we followed the gnome.

"Look, Master," Helatha said as she pointed to the far side of the room.

Toxin rapidly blinked in place within a single teleporter, frozen in time and seemingly stuck. Was it a trap, or had one of them malfunctioned? I had no way to repair the teleporter if it was the latter. If it were the former, Toxin was our resident expert on traps, yet he was the one ensnared.

"Oh, look...it says, 'Every journey forward begins with a step,'" Carine said as she read the first plaque, which was mounted on a pedestal near a single teleportation platform.

"Careful. We don't know how this is set up. We could all become frozen like Toxin," I warned. The gnome's impetuousness and curiosity could end up getting us into trouble.

"I've seen floors like this in other dungeons. Sometimes the key is to figure out the pattern," Carine said as she looked around the room.

"Some of these are flickering as if their enchantments are weak, and Toxin appears to be trapped. We may not be able to approach this problem as it was intended," I said.

"We'll just have to be extra careful," Carine said as she continued to analyze the situation.

"This is too dangerous for any of us to attempt. We could become trapped or worse," I said after analyzing the room further. I recalled tales of malfunctioning teleporters completely disintegrating victims, or other stories where victims had lost limbs or had been combined with unseen organisms such as insects.

"Perhaps I can be of assistance, Master," Helatha offered. Opening her bag, she removed a flat disk of stone from her backpack and gently set it on the ground. Bringing her arms together, the runes imprinted in her flesh flared. A decayed hand reached out from the disk, followed by another. One of the soul snatcher's ghouls slowly pulled itself up from the summoning stone.

"I brought along several servants just for this purpose," she explained as the ghoul finally emerged completely. It was one of the common undead, not the armored ones we used to defend the church. "As you can see, they would be difficult to summon during a battle due to the slow speed in which they emerge. A side effect of using summoning stones instead of their consecrated earth."

I hadn't been aware it was possible to store the ghouls in summoning objects. Such an ability could prove to be extremely useful.

"Okay, from what I can determine, just have him stand on the teleportation stone," Carine said as she wrote a few calculations into a notebook.

Helatha looked to me instead. "What is your command?"

"Let's try it her way," I said.

The ghoul shambled forth and stepped onto the teleporter. Nothing happened.

Carine scratched her head as she turned her notes sideways. "Hmm, perhaps if he walked backward..."

"Or perhaps if we stepped on *this* stone first?" I said as I pressed down on a slightly elevated switch to the left of the teleporter. The ghoul disappeared and instantly reappeared on a small island on the far side of the massive room.

"It looks safe enough," Carine said.

Staring across the long distance, it was hard to determine any details about the undead warrior. "Is it unharmed, Helatha?"

She closed her eyes. "I can detect no damage to it. It seems to be functioning properly."

"Gogbog, you will need to separate yourself from the harness so that you and Xagrim can step through separately," I said.

One by one we followed the ghoul through and arrived at the small island. Another display greeted us, along with two teleportation stones and two activation stones. The activation stones had three wavy lines on one and a mountain on the other carved upon them.

"Interesting, this script is in Nosteran. It says, 'Which is stronger: a breeze or a mountain?'" I said.

"What an easy riddle, obviously a mountain!" Carine said as she moved to press the stone with the symbol of a mountain on it.

"Wait!" I said, but it was too late. "Do not press them again without my input."

"But...isn't a mountain stronger than a breeze?" Carine asked.

"The Nosteran desert was formed by massive mountains that were eroded over thousands of years. I believe the text was in Nosteran for a reason," I explained.

"What happens if we choose wrong?"

"Helatha," I said as I gestured toward the teleporter. The ghoul obediently stepped through the device and reappeared where we had started. After stepping on the starting stone and reactivating the initial teleporter, he rejoined us.

"So, it's not as bad as it seems. It looks like most of these have only two or three choices, and we just pick the other answer if we get it wrong," Carine said. "It's not like we're dropped into the cavern below or hit with a fireball."

"Look again, fool," Helatha said as she pointed toward the display. The riddle had changed.

"'The end of days, begins anew,'" Carine read aloud. "Wait, there are three stones now!"

Indeed, an additional stone had risen from the floor in addition to the other two. One contained the symbol for Negath, the God of Death, one a symbol for Hialia, the Goddess of Life, and the third the symbol for Temphorus, the God of Time.

"Obviously it's Negath," Carine said as she moved toward the stone.

"Stop. Negath might mean the end, but there is no rebirth or a new beginning according to his scripture. His final reign means the end of all existence. It's Temphorus. Legend says our calendar is based on his designs. Once the end of five hundred days is reached, a new year begins," Helatha said.

"Are they all going to be as tedious as this?" Carine asked. "We've wasted twenty minutes and we've only moved to one new section."

I frowned. "I'm afraid so. This is why I despise puzzles."

"But you're so good at them! We'll be through this in no time!" Carine said as she pressed the correct stone. This time the ghoul appeared on an L-shaped platform a hundred feet away from us.

So it went for the next hour, as we moved from platform to platform. Between Helatha, Carine, and I, we possessed enough knowledge to answer most of the riddles correctly. On one riddle concerning the stages of the life cycle of a tree, I answered incorrectly, and we lost the ghoul as it was sent back to the start. Or rather, I answered correctly, and the riddle's answer had been incorrect. It seemed the person who had created the riddles had done so long ago, and our knowledge as a society had progressed since those many years ago. Due to the "correct" answer, I guessed the riddles had been generated over two centuries ago.

Unfortunately, there was no way to get the ghoul through the puzzles as we couldn't see what the new riddles were for him. We left him at the beginning. Helatha retrieved another summoning disk and produced a second ghoul.

I was surprised we hadn't made it to the platform on which Toxin was trapped by now. Had the rogue actually answered this many riddles correctly? I hadn't thought he'd been a learned man when he was alive, but perhaps I'd assumed incorrectly.

"Wait...send your first ghoul through the teleporter again," I said.

"What's that going to do?" Carine asked.

"I simply want to test something that just occurred to me."

Helatha mentally commanded the ghoul onto the teleportation stone. This time, he appeared on the opposite side of the room from where it had taken him and us before.

"But...why did that happen?" Helatha asked.

"We assumed it would always take us back to that initial platform if we had to start over, but I believe it may be random. That first time he ended up back on the same island as us was just a coincidence. He could have ended up anywhere. If we miss an answer and have to start over, we may end up on any one of these platforms and have to start again. I believe that's why Toxin is where he is. It's not that he answered dozens of riddles correctly, that's just the first random platform he ended up on when he stepped on the first teleporter. Although he could have answered a few correctly for all we know."

"How do we get to the door, then?" Carine asked.

"We most likely have to answer a certain number of riddles correctly, or perhaps there is a pattern to it all..." I said as I analyzed our path thus far. If there had been a pattern, I didn't see it. It looked as if we'd been on almost every island. "Perhaps we merely have to set foot on every platform before we can exit."

As luck would have it, our next jaunt took us to Toxin's location. The rogue blinked in and out of existence, frozen in place. That's when I noticed he held a particular object in his hand — the artifact Nebulus had used to instantly overcome my own puzzle wall. "So that's what happened. He attempted to cheat the system," I said. "Perhaps it short circuited the magic and created this loop."

"He's fortunate to be in one piece. Teleportation magic is not something to be trifled with," Helatha warned.

"How do we get him out? For that matter, how do we move on?" Carine asked.

Helatha and I looked at each other, then back to Toxin. I looked to Gogbog. The elderly goblin shrugged.

"Leave him. He is lost to us. He was foolish and paid the price," Xagrim said.

"Even if we were going to do that — which we aren't — we need to use the teleporter to move to the next platform, Xagrim," I said as I looked over the teleportation stone. "We need to generate a massive amount of magic near the stone without damaging it. That should short it out."

"Then how will we move on?" Carine asked.

"As soon as Toxin is free, if I pour enough magic into the stone, it should reactivate the link, just as Publin and I did to the stone upstairs."

"The problem lies in the fact none of us possess a single spell powerful enough to overcome the stone's protections. It took a master wizard's top-tier spell to break the link on the stone you speak of, Master," Helatha said.

I nodded in agreement. "Yes, but combined, we do possess enough power. Between you, Gogbog, and myself, we should be able to provide an overload of magic equal to Elemental Lord Yolune's spell."

Helatha looked thoughtful for a moment. "Yes, I believe it could work. Our timing will have to be precise, and we need to avoid striking the stone itself or we could damage it."

"Do you understand what we are doing, Gogbog?" I asked the elderly shaman.

He slowly looked from me to Helatha to the teleporter before nodding. I wondered if he would have the speed we needed to coordinate our casting. Perhaps if he summoned a powerful totem, we could channel our magic into it. The resultant destruction of the totem would release a strong burst of magic.

"I want Gogbog to summon a lightning totem to the left of the teleportation stone. On the count of ten, Helatha and I will immediately strike it with two strong spells," I said. "Carine, begin the countdown."

Gogbog nodded before he began waving his staff around and chanting. I began summoning my own magic as Helatha also started casting. Gogbog's totem appeared several seconds before Carine finished her countdown, only to be struck by a massive fireball and a black bolt of energy seconds later. The totem exploded, sending bolts of lightning, corrupt energy, and flame flying in all directions. The shockwave sent us staggering back several steps. Gogbog fell backward, but Xagrim steadied him before he hit the ground.

When the smoke cleared, Toxin was nowhere to be found. The smell of burnt hair and fabric filled the air.

"Um...wasn't he supposed to be freed?" Carine said as she looked around the room.

Indeed, Toxin was missing. I ordered my orb of light down into the abyss around us, but there seemed to be no end to it. Had we blown him over the edge, or had he been vaporized when we'd forced the device to malfunction? Unfortunately, there was no time to investigate.

Kneeling, I placed my hand on the still-hot teleportation stone and felt for the sister stone. Observing the newly severed link between them floating in the ether, I poured a portion of my magic into the device. With a spiritual "clink," the bond between the two stones was reestablished.

"I don't see him anywhere," Carine said as she scanned the area with a ridiculously large telescope.

"He may be gone. Once we figure our way through these riddles, I'll try and determine if I have enough magic in the portable sphere to resurrect him," I said. "The teleporter should be repaired."

"Let's go!" Carine said as she prepared to enter the device.

"Wait!" I cried as I grabbed her cloak and jerked her back. I pointed toward the pedestal. "We have not solved the riddle yet."

She blushed and chuckled nervously. "Why...so you're right. That would have been something if I'd ended up back at the start. We'd have to start all over again!"

"Would we?" Helatha asked.

"I mean...you wouldn't leave me...all alone...would you?"

Instead of answering, I focused on the riddle before us. Four stones held the engraved images of water, fire, stone, and air. Written on the pedestal was, "Necessary for life."

"I think...water? I don't think the others are necessary...unless you're a stone elemental or a bird, right?" Carine asked.

"There are birds that do not fly, and the stone elemental you mentioned does not require water," Helatha countered.

Carine put her hand to her chin and stroked it. "But is it really alive? Do they eat or reproduce? I think they simply crumble into smaller rocks when they reproduce, and those grow to new elementals, right?"

"In this instance, none of that matters. You're speaking of modern knowledge, not what was believed centuries ago. If my estimation of the time period these riddles were produced is correct, there is only one possible answer," I said as I stepped on the water stone, then each of the other three in succession. "It was once believed that all life came from the four elements, that they combined in certain ways to create an elemental, or a human, or a dragon. Of course, our knowledge today is more advanced, but that information wouldn't have been available so long ago," I said as I motioned for Helatha to send the ghoul through.

After a flash of light, the ghoul reappeared on a ledge to our right. Each of us followed suit and gathered on the ledge.

"Hey, there's no puzzle or teleporter!" Carine exclaimed after a quick search of the area.

"Perhaps this is a trap, or the teleporter malfunctioned," Helatha said as she began running her fingers along the smooth stone wall.

I searched the area along with the others. My concern grew that we'd somehow damaged the teleporter and ended up trapped on the ledge. The nearest island was thirty feet away. Could one of us somehow make the jump? Perhaps if Xagrim threw Carine...

A rumbling sound indicated something had been triggered. Had one of us inadvertently tripped a hidden mechanism? We grouped up and backed away as Xagrim stood between us and the sound. A rectangle pushed out from the wall and slid to the side, revealing a doorway. Toxin stood on the other side, looking perplexed.

"Apologies, Master. I am not sure how I ended up here," the rogue said. "I've inspected the rest of this passage and it is free of obstacles. The door down is open — this level does not have a key."

"Why did he travel to that side of the wall, and we ended up over here?" Carine said as we followed Toxin down the hall.

"My guess is the surge in power when the teleporter was overloaded either sent him too far, and he should have appeared where we appeared, or when we re-energized the teleporter, it was too weak to teleport us the full distance," I said. Perhaps the ledge was meant to allow for a ranged warrior or magic user to attack people as they solved the puzzles. Then they could retreat through the door Toxin had opened and flee to the floor below.

After a short walk, we reached the top of the stairwell leading down to the next level.

"That was extremely annoying," Helatha remarked as she stored the second ghoul back into its stone disk. The undead creature stood upon the plate then slowly sank away until it was gone from sight. She apparently had no concern over the one we left behind.

"Indeed," I agreed. I'd rather face dozens of monsters over puzzles and traps.

Carine folded her arms in a defensive posture. "I thought it was fun! Like a trivia contest at an inn!"

"We wasted over three valuable hours in that room. Even if the level had been filled with monsters, we probably would have completed it sooner," I said. "We should make haste to the next level."

Toxin paused and handed me the magical lock-picking device. "This would be more suited for your talents. I do not want to see it again," he said as he turned to follow the others down the stairwell.

Thinking back to his flickering form trapped in the teleporter, I chuckled. It was the closest I'd ever seen something approaching an apology or admission of folly on the rogue's part. Stowing the artifact in my satchel, I stepped through the doorway leading down.

CHAPTER SIXTEEN
Refuse

Halfway down the steps, the smell of methane and sulfur wafting up from below became nearly unbearable.

"It smells like a sewer," Carine said as she held her nose.

"Douse your torch," I said.

She looked over the edge of the stairwell. "Why? Is something coming? Should we hide...oh wait, you mean..."

"An explosion is coming if you continue down with an open flame. From this point forward, no one is to use any flame, heat, electrical magic, or items. The staff said this level contains the remnants of a sewer system. I'd thought any waste material would have dissipated or rotted away by now, but the scents we are smelling prove otherwise."

"A...sewer?" Carine said as her brow furrowed.

"Yes. Is that a problem?"

"No, it's not...a problem," Carine said sheepishly. "It's just...with my height..."

"I go where you lead, Master," Helatha said, as if proving it was no problem for her.

"If we end up wading through chest-high sewage, you can ride on my shoulders," I promised.

The gnome appeared relieved, while Helatha frowned intently.

The landing room came into sight. Xagrim continued unabated, seemingly oblivious to the smell and gases around us, while I held the rest of the group back as something began to concern me. "Xagrim! Return to us quickly!" I shouted.

He reversed course and stomped up the steps as I led the party to higher ground. Reaching into a satchel I'd designated for medical treatments, I pulled out a small ampule of smelling salts. "Turn around, Xagrim." I said.

Gogbog's unconscious body flopped about as Xagrim turned. The smelling salts resuscitated the elderly goblin in seconds as I gently patted the side of his face.

"Sleep?" he asked groggily.

"What happened to him?" Helatha asked.

"Xagrim and Toxin are immune to gases and poison, but we are not. Below a certain level, the fumes are too powerful. We won't be able to breathe freely on this level," I explained.

"I don't have any spells or prayers that would allow us to travel through such conditions," Helatha said.

"Such spells are beyond my current spellcasting level as well," I admitted. There were spells that had been specifically designed to counter such hostile environments, but I would require much more practice and study before they would become available for use. This was one area where a more experienced group would have helped.

"Know answer," Gogbog said as he pointed up the stairwell.

I knew the shamans and druids had spells that would allow people to breathe and swim underwater; perhaps Gogbog knew of one that would allow us to travel through the poisonous gases of the sewer system.

Once reaching the upper floor, Xagrim set the shaman down. The old goblin immediately removed a few items from his bag and motioned for Carine to approach him. "Make so can go below," the shaman said.

"I'm not sure...what are you going to do?" she asked with suspicion.

"Hush," he answered as he sprinkled powder from his medicine bag over her. He began chanting in a low tone, but his voice rose as he swung his staff over his head. This was the most animated I'd ever seen the old goblin since we'd started. Finally, it seemed his ritual had reached a crescendo. "Ghoojoo!" he shouted as he tapped the end of his staff to the gnome's head.

In a puff of smoke, Carine was gone — or so it seemed. Her gear was scattered on the floor and inside her clothing something struggled to free itself. I leaned over and cautiously pulled back her cloak, revealing a massive green frog.

It hopped free of its clothing and looked up at us. "Ribbit?" it asked as it attempted to figure out what had happened. Upon hearing its own voice, it croaked again. "Ribbit?" it said as it held out its webbed feet and stared at them in shock. The frog cast an accusing glare at Gogbog and shouted in indignation, "Ribbit!"

Helatha grinned evilly at the newly formed amphibian. "I much prefer her this way. I could carry her in my backpack...or we could simply leave her here," the soul snatcher said.

"How does this help us get through the sewer, Gogbog?" I said as I stifled a laugh. Carine hopped about angrily as if looking for someone to attack.

"Sludge Frog, no poison," Gogbog explained as if he didn't understand why we were confused, and Carine was upset at having been reduced to a frog.

"How would we defend ourselves and carry our gear if we were frogs?" I asked.

The shaman looked thoughtful for a moment before shrugging. "Give to metal man?"

For a second, I considered the idea, but leaving Xagrim and Toxin to defend us while we were helpless didn't seem like an ideal solution. What if something happened to Gogbog and we spent the rest of our days hopping around a sewer?

Carine bounced up and down as if trying to tell us something.

"I think she's suffered enough. Change her back, please," I said.

Gogbog shrugged and began waving his staff again.

Helatha grabbed the shaman's staff. "Perhaps there's some merit to the shaman's idea..." she pleaded.

"No, Helatha. We are not leaving her a frog," I said.

She let go of the staff and folded her arms defensively. "Very well, Master."

Again, Gogbog performed his ritual as before. Upon tapping the frog with his staff, he shouted, "Uggbug!" In another puff of smoke, Carine now stood before us.

"Why you...what made you think I'd want to be a slimy disgusting frog? I'm not some lab experiment, you know! I've never been so humiliated in all my life! If King Therion wasn't here,

I'd have a good mind to knock you flat on your —" she rattled off without pausing for a breath. Then she noticed the looks on our faces.

"What are you all staring at? What's so funny?" she said as she followed Helatha's bemused gaze. I averted my eyes out of respect.

Slowly, the infuriated gnome looked down. "I'm nude!" she shrieked as she dashed toward her clothes and gathered them up, so they covered her exposed naughty bits. "Turn around and stop staring, you evil hag!" she shouted as she dressed herself behind Xagrim's massive legs.

"I haven't been this amused in ages," Helatha said as she began to laugh at the flustered gnome.

Gogbog scratched his head as if he didn't understand any of what was happening.

"I've a good mind to just...oh, I'm so mad!" Carine stammered as she stormed back to the group.

"Calm yourself, Carine. We apologize for your...discomfort," I said with a stone face. Inwardly, I was laughing more than Helatha.

"Well, as long as you apologize...I guess I'll let you use the devices I packed specifically for this situation," she said as she began searching one of her many satchels. She paused and cast Helatha one last withering glare before pulling out a translucent helmet.

"This is the Helmeted Atmosphere Tool, or H.A.T.," Carine said as she slipped the bowl over her head. Around the base, an air-filled bladder inflated, creating a seal against the gnome's body. "In addition to a small internal air tank, it's got a magic filter that can recycle air, so you've got around two hours of air supply."

"I suppose that's fine for you, but what about the rest of us?" Helatha asked.

Carine produced three more, handing one to each of us. "I brought a few for the other two as well, but since they don't need to breathe, it's a moot point. I've used these on a few other adventures when we have to go into underwater areas."

"This is why I chose to invite you," I said as I inspected the device. It was a remarkable design. Removing my helm, I stowed it in a satchel before lowering the massive globe over my head. The seal instantly closed tight.

The petite gnome blushed at the praise. "It's was nothing...you should see the second version I'm working on."

"Why didn't you speak up about these before? You could have saved yourself the embarrassment," Helatha asked.

"I thought he was going to cast some kind of breathing spell on us! Not transform me into an amphibian!" Carine protested. "These things cost a lot of money, so I don't pull them out unless it's absolutely necessary."

"If they are damaged, the kingdom will reimburse you — with interest," I promised.

The gnome smiled and patted me on the arm. "Gee, there are some real benefits to adventuring with the king!"

"Indeed, there are. Now, let us continue to the next level and get into and out of it as quickly as possible. Two hours is not a lot of time, and I'm sure we will not want to expose ourselves longer than necessary to whatever contaminants exist below."

Upon reaching the landing room level, we each took exploratory breaths. Carine's helmets proved effective against the gases that lingered, which was a relief. Traveling through the level as a frog in Xagrim's sack sounded like a death sentence. If we were successful in our mission, I swore to learn some spells to protect against harsh environments. The question at the moment was: why were there still poison gases hundreds of years after humans had used the system, and in such concentrations?

I summoned an extra orb of light as we moved out of the room to compensate for the loss of torches. The walls of the level were slimy, slick, green stone. Raised walkways lined the base of each wall, then dropped off into fetid, black and green liquid several feet below. Bubbles slowly emerged from the surface of the substance and popped with a belch, as if the ooze were giving birth. The air was clouded with green fog.

Bending down, I touched the tip of a dagger to the surface of the substance. When I drew it back, a long trail of viscous slime followed. "I would recommend avoiding physical contact with this. Which way is the key, Carine?"

"I think it's…this way," she said as she waved her sensor back and forth. We continued along the walls in the direction she'd indicated.

The floors were slick with ooze in certain spots, requiring caution. One misstep would send an unwary adventurer flailing into the black slime. Despite the multiple orbs of light, the green fog limited visibility to perhaps a few dozen feet.

Belches and burps from the river of disgusting slime surprised us periodically, sounding as if something was rising from the ooze.

"I imagine nothing could live in this filth. I don't expect we'll find anything alive on this entire level," I said. If the air was this toxic, I was sure the liquid around us couldn't support any aquatic wildlife.

Xagrim paused. "There's something ahead." The giant death knight unsheathed his sword and strode forth, seemingly unconcerned for his own safety.

"Stop," I ordered. "Remember — you have a passenger. Do not fling yourself so callously into combat, Xagrim."

His glowing blue eyes flared at the rebuke, but he lowered his weapon. I squeezed by him, my armor scraping against the disgusting stone wall. As I moved past, my line of sight was blocked by the knight's massive weapon. I recalled facing that sword in the Dire Hall as it crashed into the floor, sparks and stone erupting wherever the heavy blade struck.

"Wait...we can't use our weapons in here. Keep them sheathed," I said.

"What if we are attacked?" Xagrim boomed.

"If our weapons strike the floors or walls, it could generate a spark and incinerate us all," I explained as I moved ahead of Xagrim. I then caught the movement he'd detected. Something approached along the ledge we were traveling, although it moved slowly and looked to be of no threat. I willed one of the orbs to travel to meet it.

A small black mound of ooze moved forward a foot at a time, pausing a few seconds between movements. Once the orb of light drew close enough, the creature stopped, as if blinded or startled. It reminded me of one of the gloobs from the dungeon, but slightly larger.

"It's merely a slime," I said. Of course, such creatures could exist in a harsh environment such as this. In fact, many types thrived in such lethal places.

"Err...I don't want to alarm anyone, but there's one back here, too," Carine called from the rear of the group.

"More than one," Toxin said as he appeared on the ledge across from us. The rogue began removing the vials of poison built into his dagger handles and searching through his armor's interior pockets.

"How many?" I asked. Even a dozen of the creatures would present little threat due to their speed. Depending on the type, slimes usually attacked by either engulfing their opponents or lashing at them with tendrils. Both attacks were slow and usually without much force. While deadly to pests such as rats and roaches, humans were rarely harmed by the unusual creatures.

"Hundreds," Toxin said as he reattached two new vials.

I could now see dozens of dark shapes slithering toward our position. "How much farther, Carine?" I said as I moved forward and kicked the first slime off the ledge.

"I think it should be up around that bend," she said as she moved away from the slimes moving up behind us.

"But we still do not know where the door is, Master," Helatha said as we quickened our pace. Toxin leapt across the river of goop and joined us, kicking away any slimes that drew too close to Carine and Helatha.

Xagrim and I had our hands full, as a few slithering blobs had turned into many. As we slung and kicked them away, they began to stick to our arms and legs, weighing us down until we could remove them. While the death knight's strength and stamina seemed limitless, I would grow tired if this continued.

"Guys, I think we have another problem..." Carine said as we fought through the voracious gelatinous nuisances.

Helatha kicked away a tendril that had wrapped around her leg. "Not now, gnome!"

"I mean, this is a *big* problem!" Carine shouted. "Look at the river!"

Casting a glance to the left, I now saw what she meant. The river's level had started to rise. Another foot and it would overflow onto the ledge we were on.

"Move faster!" I shouted as I kicked several of the monsters back into the river. Even if we could use our swords, they would prove ineffective against the formless blobs.

We passed numerous side tunnels blocked off by thick rusted grates as well as tunnels that disappeared into darkness. Without Carine's device, we could have wandered this level for hours. A small part of me wanted to explore the labyrinthine network simply to see what it contained. Perhaps if we survived, I would return, armed with the necessary spells or equipment to deal with the slimes. Could beings of such low intelligence be controlled as I controlled the skeletons and ratzgors? We'd find out.

"Right around this bend, I think!" Carine shouted as she jumped over a slime that had climbed over the ledge from the river.

Even if we managed to get the key, there was still the matter of finding the door that led to the next level. Yet, as we ran to the end of the tunnel, even obtaining the key looked to be an impossibility.

"What...is that?" Helatha whispered as our group paused in awe of the spectacle before us.

Every surface of the tunnel in front of us pulsated with strands of black slime stretched and tethered to the walls and ceiling. The river merged into one gargantuan blob that was big enough to engulf a small home. Tentacles thrashed about, slapping into the walls with wet *swacks* that sounded as if they could cave in a man's ribcage. From those tentacles, large drops were flung to the ground, then forming an unending stream of slimes that oozed down the walkways toward us.

"Helatha, do you have any elemental-based protection spells or prayers?" I asked.

"I-I think I know a minor protection prayer," the soul snatcher stammered as she fought to pull her eyes away from the abomination in front of us.

"Cast it on the entire party," I said as I punted a few more slimes back into the roiling mass that spawned them.

"Xagrim — there's only one thing we can do against this creature," I said as I cast several ice darts at some of the smaller tentacles, which froze and shattered. Xagrim set Gogbog down and moved away from the group.

A wave of cold rushed out from the death knight as frost began to coat his armor. Toxin leapt to the front just as Helatha's prayer finished. I could feel her protective spell reduce the cold coming from Xagrim, but it would need to get much colder if we were going to have a chance against the monstrosity.

The three of us rushed into reach of the creature's tentacles. Using my shield, I blocked or slammed them away, while also flattening as many of the smaller creatures as I could. Darts of icy cold froze the areas they hit, but the damage seemed minimal as fresh slime simply rolled over the frozen bits.

Toxin's daggers darted into the blob as the rogue ducked and flipped over and around tentacles that attempted to swat him. Any area he jabbed froze and melted away into a watery liquid bereft of life.

Xagrim waded into the mass, knocking away the creature's appendages with his armored fists. Each blow he struck iced over the creature's flesh, causing it to crumble. One tentacle wrapped around the death knight's torso, lifting him from his feet, but it slowed and broke to pieces before it could toss him down the tunnel or bash him against a wall.

Gogbog summoned a totem of cold that pulsed rings of frigid magic every few seconds, freezing the slimes that menaced the group from the rear. The shaman shattered any frozen slimes with his staff.

Helatha opened her black bible, the Aeon Torment, and closed her eyes as she began praying to Castigous. A swarm of particles erupted from her mouth, blasting the slime in the river as well as any of the smaller ones that had gotten past the fighters on the front lines. Any of the slimes that came into contact with the evil particles began to wither and shrivel as if dehydrated. It could have been my imagination, but the river's level appeared to decrease slightly.

"That's a good idea!" Carine said as she searched her pouches for something to help. "Aha!" she exclaimed as she pulled out a vial of reddish crystals. "Sand hydra tears...great for quickly drying out your clothes and laundry!" The gnome began sprinkling the contents of her vial on the slimes, which turned to dust in seconds. "If only I had a whole bag of this stuff!"

Between our combined efforts, the creature seemed to at least partially weaken. Then again, after only a few minutes of battle, Xagrim's armor held several new dents, and I was sure I had more deep bruises and welts across the areas not protected by my metal armor. Progress was slow, but if we could continue at our current pace, victory was achievable. That's when it fell apart.

A massive tentacle rose from the river, sneaking behind Toxin and grabbing the nimble rogue from behind. In a split second, it dashed him against the wall then pulled him down into the river of slime. The creature's attacks redoubled, pummeling Xagrim and I with renewed vigor.

"I think I see him!" Carine said as she peered over the edge. A figured coated with slime reached up for assistance. The memory of Ho'Scar's slime pit trap in his torture chamber sprang to mind. Before I could move to help him, Toxin was dragged under again.

While the king slime had diminished in size, we were now down a valuable group member, while the others were tiring quickly.

"Helatha and Carine — clear a path behind us," I shouted. "We're retreating!"

"But what about your friend?" Carine asked as she slung crystals across a mass of slimes.

"Just do as I say!" I yelled. "I need two frost totems near Xagrim, Gogbog!"

The elderly shaman's eyebrows rose slightly, but he did as he was instructed.

"Xagrim, grab those totems!" I shouted as I launched single ice darts to cover the knight. Two tentacles froze solid just above him as he leaned down to grab the pulsing magical totems.

"Now, fight!"

Xagrim looked down at his hands, then punched through the two tentacles, shattering them to pieces. Each of his sub-zero strikes radiated pulses of frigid cold that froze everything around him instantly right before his nearly impenetrable fists of steel struck and shattered his enemies.

The waves of cold and frost wafted down the sewer system behind him, leaving us chilled to the bone despite Helatha's minor enchantments. Just as we retreated farther, a humanoid form burst from the slime river that had yet to be frozen by Xagrim's cold fury.

Snatching Gogbog's staff, I leaned out and offered it to the slime-coated rogue. His hands slipped along the length of the staff, unable to find purchase.

Aiming for the area behind his legs, I launched another ice dart, which solidified the slime enough for Toxin to kick out of it. Once safely on the ledge, I rolled him away from the river and propped him up against the wall.

Analyzing the state of the massive slime, I pulled Nebulus' spellbook from my satchel and began reciting a spell I'd recently added to my repertoire. Timing would mean everything.

"Grahh!" Xagrim's hollow voice rang out as he ripped through the creature, digging his way deeper with each frigid strike. After several more blows, over seventy percent of the monster was frozen solid, along with the river leading away from it.

The already difficult spell was made more difficult by my shivering hands and chattering teeth. "M-move away from it,

Xagrim!" I shouted as I launched a wave of force to the left of the knight. The force bolt splattered the unfrozen area of the slime into droplets, but the damaged area quickly refilled. Several seconds later, a second bolt hit the same spot, but this time the damage had doubled, leaving a much deeper divot in the monster. The third blast exploded the area into a mist of slime droplets.

By now, Xagrim had clambered away from the creature, leaving three quarters of it frozen solid.

The next two bolts of force ripped the remaining creature to shreds, sending frozen slime shards and particles bouncing around the cell like exploded shrapnel. Fortunately for us, the second component of the spell included a shield of force that protected us from the brunt of the dangerous projectiles.

Carine pushed herself up from the slime-covered ground. "We...we did it! It's gone!"

"The Master did it, you did nothing," Helatha said.

"I helped, you old hag! At least as much as you did," Carine argued.

Surveying the chamber, it became obvious this creature could reform if given enough time once the ice melted. Several globs of it were already inching toward each other. Xagrim stomped out any he came across.

I pointed to the mess in front of us, which should have contained our target. "Stop bickering. Where is the key, Carine? Remember, our air supply is limited."

The gnome huffed, but retrieved the device from her bag, using it to scan the room while she moved about. After a few moments, she reached into a big glob of slime and fished around until she produced the key. "I've got the k — holy

Zoustero, look at that!" she said as she stared past Xagrim with a shocked expression on her face.

I moved one of the orbs of light to the area she faced. Flecks of gold and scintillating gems reflected the light back. The beast had amassed quite a large pile of treasure underneath its body over the centuries.

"May I?" Carine asked as she inched closer.

"Take whatever you wish. If we conquer these dungeon levels and gain control of the new Soul Sphere, I should be able to return at my leisure and rifle through the treasure even after the beast has reformed," I said.

Carine squealed with delight before leaning over the edge of the platform in an attempt to grab something of worth without falling into the frozen mass of slime below.

"Is everyone well?" I asked.

Helatha nodded. Gogbog sat in a puddle of slime and rested, his chest heaving as he attempted to catch his breath. Xagrim walked past, seemingly content at having unleashed his fury upon a worthy foe. Toxin merely rested against the wall, the slime still clinging to every surface of his body. All of us looked as if we could do with a long bath.

Following Carine to the edge end of the tunnel, I incanted, "Desicry Arcenarum."

A few visible items glowed faintly, revealing they were enchanted. I grabbed a thin necklace chain that glowed a bit brighter than the other baubles. Perhaps buried somewhere in the muck was something of potent magical value, but it would take workers a day or longer to blockade off the river of slime and clean up the treasure so it could be cataloged.

A quick identification spell revealed the necklace was imbued with an enchantment to increase the strength of its wearer slightly, but I was surprised when a second row of information appeared under the first, stating it also increased the magic pool of its owner. It was rare to find artifacts with dual enchantments, and even rarer still where a person would pay to have enchantments that benefited physical fighters as well as magic users.

Slipping it on, I could feel the slight increase in power in both my sinews and magical reserves.

"Well, I didn't find a ruby, but maybe I can trade this emerald for something," Carine said as she inspected a fairly large gem with a jeweler's loupe. A beep sounded from her helm. "We've got to get moving! There's only twenty-five minutes of air left, and we don't even know where the door is!"

"Calm yourself. Can we not simply return to the previous level and refill our tanks, then explore this level until we find the door?" I asked.

"Oh, yeah! Why didn't I think of that? I have the pump right here!"

"Gather your belongings, we are heading back to the previous level," I announced.

The trip back went far quicker, as we knew the way and we weren't slowed by constant slime attacks. The level still crawled with them, but it seemed they were no longer focused on us exclusively. If one happened to cross our path, it attacked, but one quick stomp from Xagrim squished it into droplets. Without the king slime commanding and generating them, the threat was minimal.

The trek back to the previous level tested our endurance, as we were already exhausted from battle. Once we eventually found the door to the next level, I hoped we did not run into any immediate danger, as we needed to rest.

"Finally!" Carine exclaimed as we exited the door to the teleporter level. At least here we didn't have to worry about anything attacking us.

"Okay, give me your helmets," the gnome inventor said as she removed a large foot pump from her bag. Hooking up a hose to the end, she pointed to Xagrim. "Pump this up and down until the needle is in the green."

The death knight stared down at the gnome as if deciding if she would be the one he stepped on instead of the pump.

"Do as she says, Xagrim," I ordered. He was the only one in the group who wasn't gasping for breath. After a few gulps of water, I lay back and stared at the ceiling. I hoped our bedding hadn't been completely fouled by the adventures on the sewer level.

The death knight began slowly working the pump as Carine gathered the helmets from each of us. I'd almost dozed off when a shriek had me on my feet, ready to face whatever threat had appeared.

Looking around, my exhausted mind noticed Xagrim, Helatha, Gogbog and Toxin…where was Carine? That's when I noticed Toxin's form bulged and stretched as he backed away from the group toward the tunnel leading down. The outline of Carine's face pushed out from inside his slimy chest, her muffled cries smothered by the mass of slime she was encased within.

"Don't let it get to the door! If it makes it down to the river, we'll never find her!" I shouted. Xagrim moved to block the door as Gogbog summoned another pulsing ice totem to block the creature's exit. The creature looked around slowly as if trying to figure out what to do.

"Grab it and freeze it!" Helatha shouted.

"No! That will surely destroy her as well!" I said. My mind raced to try and figure out a way to free the gnome from the slime. While we could use fire on this level, it would be impossible to inflict enough damage to the slime without boiling Carine alive as well. Electricity? No, the current would travel through her.

"Think...think," I whispered as the humanoid-shaped slime tottered around and began slinking toward the teleporters. Would it plummet into the abyss with Carine trapped inside?

The image of us whipping our hands and feet to sling the slime from us popped into my thoughts. "Vortexus Turbini!" I shouted as I focused on the slime creature. A small wind devil sprang up, kicking up dust throughout the room as it bore down on the hapless, slowly fleeing monster. In seconds, the howling winds enveloped the blob, spinning it quickly in place. Bits of slime splattered across the floor and into the walls as centrifugal force ripped the creature from Carine's body, bit by bit. In seconds, all that was left was a spinning, gasping gnome.

Dispelling the wind, I rushed to her and helped her to stop whirling in circles. She fell to her bottom as her head wobbled. In a daze, she asked, "What...happened?"

"It seems the slimes had one last trick to pull. They created a slime duplicate of Toxin and it attacked you, attempting to absorb you. If it had been smarter, it would have waited until we were asleep, but these creatures seem to have rudimentary intelligence," I said.

Carine looked around, her head still bobbing slightly. "Then...where's Toxin?"

CHAPTER SEVENTEEN
Mischief

After twenty minutes to refill the helmets' magic air bladders, we returned to the sewers to search for Toxin.

"I will attempt to discern his life force," Helatha said as she muttered a necromantic spell. We began walking back toward the area where we had battled the massive slime creature. After long minutes, I began to suspect he was going to be right where we had left him.

"Here," Helatha said when we were a few dozen feet downstream from where Toxin had been sucked into the slime river. "I sense something...but I do not think you will be pleased, Master."

"Xagrim," I said.

The hulking death knight knelt and plunged his massive arm into the ooze. After a few moments of feeling around, he pulled up Toxin's remnants. The skeletal rogue still held both daggers in death grips, unwilling or unable to let them go.

"Can you revive him, Master?" Helatha asked.

Pulling the portable sphere of magic from a pouch, I reached out to Toxin's life force while holding out the sphere so that I could observe it. Tentatively, I began to resurrect him, watching as over half the sphere's magic began to flicker. I let his spirit go and ceased the attempt. "No. It requires too much magic. We don't know what other obstacles we will face. If the sphere runs out, none of us will survive for much longer after that, and we certainly won't be in any condition to fight."

"You're...just going to leave him?" Carine asked.

"We'll take him with us to the level below so that the slimes...don't finish," I said.

Xagrim carried Toxin's remains as we backtracked and began searching the side tunnels for the doorway down. It would be easy to become disoriented and lost in the maze-like twists and turns, as many tunnels looked like others. We marked our paths with magical symbols so we could determine if we'd come down a certain tunnel before.

Through the process of elimination, we found the door down at the end of a tunnel that sloped upward a few degrees. The path was almost directly in the center of the main tunnel. The black slime river stopped halfway up the path, with the doorway on the right side, embedded in the moist stone wall.

Due to the elevation, the entire system would have to flood up to the ceiling before the water would possibly rise enough to meet the door. I noticed the green gases had fallen off a bit as well. Perhaps not safe enough to breathe, but not as thick as the rest of the sewer system.

Carine opened the door and we headed down the next set of steps. The thought of not having Toxin to scout and run long range interference for us made me nervous. No matter if we were captured or fell into a trap, I was confident the elite rogue would be able to get us out. Now, that assurance was lost.

"Stay here. Xagrim, follow me," I said as I opened the door out of the landing room to investigate our immediate area. There were halls that led to the left and right, which seemed unusual. Usually we were greeted by a hall leading directly ahead. After minutes of listening, I whispered a few detect magic spells every dozen feet as I left Xagrim to guard the door. Inch by inch I checked the floors, walls, and ceilings for traps or anything unusual. Detecting nothing, I continued down the hall.

The first room I encountered was a massive, luxurious bedroom the size of some of the barracks on previous levels. This room was built for nobility and had somehow been perfectly preserved. Before I could react, I felt myself falling into darkness as my head swam.

"PRINCE JAGEN, YOUR father states you must attend the ceremony to honor the soldiers returning from the war," a young female attendant said from the doorway.

Looking around the room, I was surprised by the opulence. Toys made in various countries filled almost every space. A dragon that breathed illusionary fire, a mechanical bird that flitted about the room when I called his name, swords and other weapons that looked as if they were made of steel but couldn't harm a mouse due to protective enchantments placed upon them. Paintings with gilded frames displayed acts of heroism and tales of lore. Three bookcases overflowed with books, while many open books rested on a magnificent bed and at an expensive, hand-crafted desk.

Ignoring the attendant, I walked across the room to a miniature treasure chest, about one tenth the size of a real one. Opening it, I was surprised to see it was filled with actual gold coins...more than any peasant would earn in three lifetimes.

The rug under my feet was made from a unicorn. The magical beasts had been thought to be extinct for a hundred years, hunted for the curative properties of their horns.

"What...ceremony?" I asked absently. Looking down at my hands and the difference in height between the attendant and myself, I guessed I was perhaps seven or eight.

"For the heroes that won the Battle of Titan's Spine in Nosteran. They faced a horde of Nosteran savages, outnumbered ten to one, but with Uxper's blessings, our heroes defeated those dark skin heretics. I thought you liked heroic deeds, Master Jagen?" the attendant said as she gestured toward the pictures and books around my room.

"I like...heroes..." I said absently. I felt myself falling again. This time I found myself in a small library with sandy plaster walls and a high domed ceiling. Magnificent paintings covered the entirety of the ceiling, the scenes reflecting the ancient battles between the dragons and titans, which supposedly raged eons before mankind walked the land.

Someone held my hand and pulled me toward a bookcase. Looking up, I gasped to see Aiyla racing ahead of me, dragging me along. She looked over her shoulder and smiled, her dark hair seemingly moving in slow motion.

"This is what I wanted to show you. You said you'd studied military history at the Royal Military Academy, so I thought if that interested you, I'd show you some of our records," she said.

For a moment, I didn't know how to respond. She was here, again. My old self answered, "Of course I'd like to see what your scribes have written. I've always said there's no such thing as too much knowledge."

She rolled her eyes. "Yes, your penchant for reading and study has driven me to insanity more than a few times. Recall we missed the New Year parade because you couldn't be bothered to leave the Sacred Archives on time. I could have wrung your neck for that."

"I've apologized eight times for that! Your time pieces confused me," I argued as my eyes raced over the tomes in front of us.

"Only seven, but I'll let you get away with eight," she said as she likewise began searching the shelves. The books were organized by year and title. Some concerned trade, agriculture, and engineering, but I grabbed one concerning military history.

"I should have figured," she sighed as she continued to search for something she would enjoy.

Sliding out a chair, I flipped the book open on the plain wood desk and began skimming the pages. Before long, I stumbled upon an entry — "Massacre at Titan's Spine." The date matched the one I knew from memory, concerning the clash between our two kingdoms at the historic Titan's Spine pass. It would be interesting to see how Nosteran's scribes treated Tharune's magnificent victory.

As I read, I began to grow angry at the author's interpretation of the battle. According to him, the Nosteran warriors numbered only fifty, while the Tharune forces were over five hundred. This account stated the Nosteran forces lost but managed to kill two hundred invaders before they fell by using superior tactics and the terrain against the Tharune soldiers.

Aiyla's hand reached across the table and grasped mine. "What's wrong? You look upset."

"This...is all wrong. This entry is about the Battle of Titan's Spine, and it says Tharune forces attacked a border fort within Nosteran. It states the battle was fifty against five hundred, and we still lost almost half our forces. That's not what happened at all."

"Yes, I remember that well. Our people were outraged at the slaughter. That fort was in the middle of nowhere and was there to protect ancient artifacts related to the Titan's Spine, as it was an ongoing archaeological site filled with important historical artifacts from the days of the titans. Your soldiers swooped in and attacked the fort without provocation, then looted the artifacts. It was a day of great mourning for our people."

"That-that's not what happened..." I said as I tried to recall the battle from my lessons at the Academy. "They were a military outpost...our men were heroes for overcoming thousands of Nosteran soldiers."

Aiyla shook her head. "Why would I lie? Have I ever lied to you? Why would we put a military outpost a hundred miles away from any strategic areas of interest, manned by so few people? If you studied geography, does it make any sense at all to take that outpost, unless you wanted the valuable artifacts?"

"I..." I said as I began analyzing the situation anew, disregarding what I'd learned from our history books. "No, it holds no strategic value at all. In fact, it would be a huge burden for our forces to even hold the fort, due to the distance from our supply lines."

"Exactly, my love. The only heroes that day were the ones attempting to protect those valuable historical artifacts and pieces of history and gave their lives doing so," Aiyla said as she caressed my hand.

"MASTER?" THE HOLLOW voice said from outside the bedroom. The world returned to normal as the new memories faded into the back of my mind. I recalled Aiyla's final words and wondered what other lies I'd been taught over the years.

"I'm fine, Xagrim. Simply...lost in thought," I said. Looking around the room, I realized it would make an excellent rest area for our group. Unlike the upper floors, the furniture and blankets were mostly intact and unusually clean.

"This is amazing!" Carine said as her eyes grew wide at the massive bedroom. "This almost makes up for being sucked into a slime man and being turned into a frog...almost."

"You and Helatha can take the bed. I'll sleep on the floor," I said.

"No, Master! You take the bed. You've worked the hardest of all of us and should enjoy a good night's rest," Helatha said. "The gnome is very small and would not mind sleeping on the floor, correct?"

"You...you..." Carine stammered.

"I've stated the sleeping arrangements," I said with finality. "We'll take an extra-long rest and heal completely tonight. After the battle with the slimes, we are all depleted." I pulled out a medium-sized vial filled with a red liquid, as well as one filled with a glowing blue substance. Drinking a third of the blue bottle, I passed the rest to Helatha, who drank a portion and gave the remainder to Gogbog.

Carine whistled. "That's a pricey bottle of magic potion. You don't see many of those just lying around."

"Yes, a wizard named Elemental Lord Yolune had several of them on his person, and he decided I should inherit them upon his death," I said as I sipped the red-tinted potion. The pain from my cuts and bruises faded almost immediately. Helatha and Gogbog declined, but Carine took a sip. I returned the vials to my satchel. Gogbog summoned another healing totem as I pulled out several specially prepared meat pies that I'd been saving. When Ho'Scar presented the carefully wrapped dishes to me, I could barely prevent myself from devouring them on the spot.

Pulling out a metal tripod with a flat top, Carine set it on the floor and placed a firesparker in a holder underneath it. In a moment, the top of the metal glowed red. "Just a little invention of mine that saves cooking space and time," she said with a smile.

The first pie set everyone's mouths watering before it was even fully cooked. After reheating each pie, I handed them off to everyone except Xagrim.

"Mmm! I can't believe how good this is! Was this prepared by the chefs in the castle?" Carine asked after shoveling a second huge bit into her mouth. "I imagine you eat incredible meals like this on a daily basis!"

"No, this was prepared by the dungeon's torturer. It most likely contains bits of the gnome we captured and tortured shortly before this adventure began," Helatha said.

Carine spat her food onto the floor, gagging and coughing. "G-gnome?"

"Hush, Helatha. These pies contain no humanoid flesh. It's venison," I said.

Helatha smiled wickedly at her jest. "My apologies, Master. I was simply having a bit of fun with our...diminutive friend."

Carine sniffed another spoonful and held it up to the light before she was satisfied with the nature of its contents. "Are those sweet potatoes? I haven't had those in months."

After shaking the dust from the bed covers and setting out the bedding for Gogbog and myself, we prepared to rest. Again, Xagrim would keep watch outside the door, which we kept closed and braced against intruders.

"Have you scanned for the key yet?" I asked.

Carine stopped fluffing a small pillow and retrieved her scanner. A moment later, she replied, "It's in that direction, directly in the center. I've got a strong reading on it."

"Excellent. Hopefully we can retrieve it in the morning and be on our way to the final level without much trouble," I said.

We turned down the lights and left several magical candles burning. Gogbog was asleep instantly, his long goblin nose vibrating slightly with each breath. It was more comforting than annoying, knowing another trustworthy companion slept nearby. Helatha and Carine fell asleep shortly thereafter, obviously exhausted from the massive battle in the sewer level. Sleep eluded me while I thought over our quest — the stakes and the consequences thus far.

I thought of Toxin's body, which we'd left in the landing room, covered by a blanket. I knew from experience the powerful rogue required a large amount of magic to resurrect, and the more time that passed since his death, the more magic it would take. With the Soul Sphere above leaking, and the one in my pocket slowly draining to maintain the dungeon-linked members of the group, I wondered if he was lost forever.

I thought of Zarah alone in the throne room, perhaps watching as the sphere's magic slowly ebbed away. I now realized how much I enjoyed the sound of her music constantly echoing throughout the throne room and my bedroom. I missed her wry comments and even the arguments. My eyes grew heavy as my thoughts turned to more comforting topics.

A dreamless night followed, which was unusual. Many nights I dreamed of comforting past memories, usually of Aiyla. I longed for the pleasant ones, but almost as often I was forced to experience those final days in New Vadis before she was killed.

"I've been robbed!" a voice in the darkness said. I awoke to see Carine frantically waving a torch about as she scoured the room. "Did you do something with my gauntlet, you witch? I'm *not* amused!"

Helatha summoned her own orb of light and likewise searched the room. "My Aeon Torment is missing as well. I had nothing to do with this, you nitwit."

Searching my immediate area, I noticed Purgatory was gone. I didn't see Gogbog's staff, either.

"Xagrim!" I shouted. After a moment of no answer, I whispered, "Be prepared...I'm going to open the door."

Xagrim stood motionless in the doorway, making not a sound. Had he been killed as we rested? Just as I reached out to touch him, the knight's shoulder spasmed, and he mumbled, "Fool."

"Xagrim," I said as I grabbed his shoulder. Startled, he reached for his sword, but it was gone.

"What — what is the meaning of this?" he boomed as he looked to the rest of the group for answers.

"We were hoping you could tell us that. Were you...sleeping?" I asked.

The death knight paused as if thinking. "I was asleep. I do not recall being tired, but somehow I neglected my duty during the night."

"Interesting. Did you sleep soundly, Master?" Helatha asked.

"Almost as if in a coma," I replied.

"I didn't wake up even once," Carine admitted.

"Perhaps we did not merely sleep, but were affected by a spell," Helatha offered. "Someone obviously stole our weapons but made sure we were incapacitated so that they could do so."

"We'll find them. Pack up camp and eat on the way," I said as I went back to gather up and stow my bedding.

After taking in a bit of food and taking care of other biological functions, we set off to find our missing weapons. "I have a feeling we'll find our gear when we find the key. Which way, Carine?"

"Straight ahead, toward the center of the floor."

We moved cautiously through the level, unsure of what dangers could lurk around every corner. Toxin's presence was sorely missed, but fortunately we ran into no traps. After turning left and heading down a short hall, a massive pair of doors blocked our path. The room ahead of us must have been massive, judging by the length of the halls we'd used to reach the center of the floor.

"Be prepared," I said as I nodded for Xagrim to shove the massive doors open.

The group gasped as the doors swung wide to reveal a startling sight.

"It's...beautiful!" Carine exclaimed as she crossed the threshold into the new area.

A gargantuan exquisite ballroom spread out before us. The bright red wooden floors glistened as if they'd just been polished moments ago. Banners and paintings larger than the door we'd just passed through adorned the walls. A crystalline chandelier larger than a carriage blazed with a thousand glowing lights. No light entered through the towering windows around the room, which were decorated with gold and red drapes.

Along the walls, plush couches and chairs lined with gold and leather awaited anyone who needed a respite from the festivities. The doorway we'd just come through was centered high in the wall, with golden red carpet leading down into the dance area. Colossal pillars around the room held romantic scenes such as angels and humans dancing with animals and spirits. A twenty-foot-tall fireplace on the far wall roared with a healthy fire.

"This makes no sense," Helatha said.

Indeed, the whole room glistened and sparkled as if an entire crew of servants had spent a day cleaning and polishing it. It looked as if it were ready to entertain five hundred affluent guests.

Xagrim pointed toward the center of the room. "Look, there."

Our weapons lay in a pile on the dance floor. We looked at each other before I nodded toward our items. "This is obviously a trap. Once we are on the ground floor, take up positions near cover. Xagrim and I will retrieve our weapons."

Upon reaching the floor, I moved behind Xagrim, my shield ready to deflect any spells or projectiles. The other party members took up position behind planters or columns, ready to assist if we were attacked.

As we drew closer, I cast detect magic, but found no traps in the vicinity. "It seems safe, but keep an eye out, Xagrim," I said as I gathered up our weapons. I expected as soon as my hands were full, a fireball or volley of arrows would descend upon us, but nothing happened.

After equipping ourselves, we moved toward the stairs leading out. It appeared the door we'd come through held the only exit to the room.

"Do you sense anything, Helatha?" I whispered as we neared the base of the monumental steps.

"Something's...here, but elusive," she said as she began to inspect her bible. Suddenly, she froze.

"What is it?" I asked.

She remained immobile, as if frozen in time. Carine likewise stood motionless. I turned to see if the same fate had befallen Xagrim and Gogbog but found that my body wouldn't respond.

Music began to play.

CHAPTER EIGHTEEN
Broken

Our bodies moved of their own accord toward the center of the room as we stowed our weapons. The music's volume grew louder until it seemed a full orchestra was but a dozen feet away. A haunting tune full of sorrow filled the room.

"What's happening?" Carine said as she stepped backward while facing away from Xagrim. The dour knight likewise moved away from the gnome.

Helatha and I were paired up as Gogbog moved to the side of the dance floor and began tapping his feet.

"Master, I..." Helatha said as she bowed. I returned the bow and replied, "I know." Something was possessing our bodies, and we were powerless to fight it.

The music's tempo picked up as we drew close to our partners, turning to the left, then to the right. As a group, we moved to the center and repeated the movement. Xagrim growled in frustration.

Pairing up again, Helatha and I walked past each other then reversed direction as the tempo picked up. We passed each other again, our hands brushing at the tips as we twirled away and formed a circle with Xagrim and Carine, then moved in rhythmic harmony to the beat, clapping and stamping as we moved.

"Is there any way to break this spell?" I shouted over my shoulder to Helatha.

"If only I could move my hands, I know of a dispelling magic that may work," she called back.

We broke the circle and crossed paths again, this time hooking our arms and spinning each other until we faced the opposite direction. As we spun and twirled, I frantically looked around the room for our tormentors, but it seemed we were alone.

Helatha rushed at me and I lifted her high above my head, spinning her around as she stiffened her legs and held out her arms as if she were a bird on the wing. The dark priestess looked down at me and smiled slightly at the ridiculous situation we found ourselves in. I couldn't help but grin in return, at least briefly.

Setting her down, we continued to frolic and dance for another twenty minutes. The styles of dance and the music changed three times during the performance. At last, we came together and bowed to each performer in turn before we gained possession of our bodies again. The music continued, but at a much lower volume, as if allowing the participants of the dance to mingle and talk.

"That was...interesting," Helatha said. "I believe the one responsible placed some sort of enchantment upon our weapons."

"And since they are all enchanted or related to magic, my spell didn't detect anything unusual," I said.

"That was humiliating! This big tin oaf spun me about like a top! I thought he was going to throw me out the window!" Carine huffed.

"I will dismember the ones responsible," Xagrim growled as his eyes flashed in anger.

The music stopped and the lights dimmed, except for a single beam that fell upon the center of the room. Hovering in midair was the key.

"I'm not touching it!" Carine said as she wiped the sweat from her brow and attempted to catch her breath. Gogbog sat on the floor, seemingly exhausted from merely clapping for almost half an hour.

"I'll do it," Helatha said as she moved to grab the key. The cylinder of light faded away as a faint laughter echoed from far away. We waited for the next trick or trap, but nothing happened.

"Seems someone was having a bit of fun at our expense," I said.

Helatha pulled out her black bible, closed her eyes, and concentrated as she whispered a prayer, "I do not sense a malevolent entity. It seems to be rather powerful, however."

"We should find the door before it comes back. There's no telling what it could do," I said.

"*That* door?" Carine said as she pointed to the far wall that faced the one with the fireplace.

"That wasn't there before."

As we hastened toward the newly visible door, Helatha spoke. "This is a rather curious level. A sewer above, and a room more elegant than any other in the dungeon below it."

"I've long given up hope of making sense of the dungeon's floor arrangements," I replied as I placed the key in the lock. To my relief, it opened. I half expected fireworks to erupt from the keyhole or for it to devour the key. The thick, metal door swung open.

"The following level is the last one," I said before we entered the stairwell. "If there is another Soul Sphere, it will be here."

"What can we exp —" Carine began to ask before the world shattered. Or perhaps it was my mind...or part of my soul. The sound of tinkling glass shards raining on my psyche drowned out everyone around me. A stabbing pain crushed my chest, feeling almost as if my heart were bursting.

"What's wrong with him?" I heard a voice say, but it sounded as if it were underwater.

"It's lost..."

"Who's there?" I called out to the new, familiar voice.

"J-Jagen?"

"Zarah? Where are you? What is happening?"

"Gone..." she said as her voice echoed in the darkness. It sounded as if she were traveling farther away with each word. "Dying..."

It felt as she were slipping away, unable to continue speaking. I focused my will on her, reaching out into the ether to find her. Just as it seemed she was beyond my grasp, I felt her weak presence. I grabbed for anything.

In the darkness, I then saw my hand as it found hers. She appeared before me as if pulled up from a dark pit into the light.

"Jagen? I-I'm sorry," she said as we stood in the nothing space.

"What has happened?"

"They came...more of them. I couldn't stop them. It was just as before...they completely destroyed the Soul Sphere," she cried. "I'm fading..."

"Come," I said as I willed myself back to reality while concentrating on Zarah.

Carine's face loomed over me, blocking my view. "Are you okay?"

"I'm fine," I said as I stood. "Zarah."

Zarah materialized beside us. "H-how?"

"I willed you to join me."

"But the Soul Sphere is shattered, I thought..."

I pulled out the portable sphere. Its magic level had dropped around ten percent since the last time I'd observed it. It was slightly over half full. "As long as we have this, we can continue on. I suppose you are linked to this one now. What happened? How did invaders get by the soldiers?"

"They came through the goblin teleporter. I sensed them right away, but just as before, they were hidden from my view. I found several dead goblins in their wake, but it seems they purposely avoided the creatures in the dungeon and headed directly for the Soul Sphere. There was nothing I could do to slow them down. There were six of them this time."

I was shocked to hear that the intruders had come through the teleporter. Had they destroyed the goblin village? Did their mysterious control over our forces extend to outside the dungeon?

"We should be able to reach the next Soul Sphere before they arrive if they just destroyed the one above," I said.

"No...five of them began their descent a day ago, while one remained behind for some reason. They have a head start," Zarah said.

"A day...?" I wondered if their ability to control or evade the dungeon's guardians extended to the deeper levels. Either way, we'd cleared many of the obstacles for them. They also had the advantage of somehow being able to sense the doors and keys, and the enchantments on the current doors were so weak, even if they were locked, a sufficiently powerful group could break through in perhaps twenty or thirty minutes. The strange creatures they employed could perhaps even do it instantly.

"We need to reach the Soul Sphere before engaging them," I said as I turned to descend the stairwell. "I just hope we have the power to defeat what waits for us as well as these new enemies."

Carine grabbed my arm before asking, "What's waiting below? You haven't told us yet."

I thought back to what the staff had told me before we ventured into the wild dungeon's depths.

"Be wary of the final level. It will be your most difficult challenge. In fact, I don't know how you will overcome it with such meager forces. A dragon guards the next Soul Sphere."

CHAPTER NINETEEN
Inevitable

Carine sputtered as we inched down the steps. "A-a dragon? I mean...a dragon?"

"A dragon," I repeated for the third time.

"On one hand, I've never seen a real, live dragon. On the other hand, we need to defeat it to move on. I mean...it's like a wish come true, and then you die."

"We don't necessarily have to defeat it. We may be able to sneak past it — if a certain gnome would silence herself," Helatha said.

"Has it been like this the entire trip?" Zarah asked.

"Indeed."

"My sympathies. I still don't understand how you brought me here. How did you know I was in trouble?"

"I...sensed it. Then I reached out to you and found you. It's like we were linked."

"Well, I am your heart."

I cast a sideways glance at her to find her studying me. "What?"

"You...held me. I haven't felt that in a long time."

"It was...nothing. My instincts told me I needed to pull you back to the dungeon, and I did."

She grinned. "Of course."

"We...should focus on the next level. We shouldn't become distracted," I said.

"Of course."

Upon reaching the bottom of the steps, we checked ourselves over and replenished our magical reserves. Not knowing what type of dragon we'd face, we cast several elemental protections upon the group. The spell was weak, but better than nothing.

"What happened to Toxin?" Zarah asked as she changed outfits to one that looked more suited to battle.

"He fell on the previous level. I don't have enough magic to risk bringing him back."

"That's a shame. He was a powerful warrior," Zarah replied.

I was concerned about the upcoming battle with the dragon without the rogue's help. His powerful poisons and enchanted daggers could prove vital to bringing the beast down.

"Let Xagrim and I distract it while you attack from afar. If there is any way to reach the Soul Sphere while it's distracted, I'll take it," I said. "Ready?"

"Your will be done, Master," Helatha said.

Curiously, this level's layout reminded me of the level that contained the throne room and Dire Hall. One extremely long hall made up of polished black stone. Unlike some of the previous levels, this one was pitch black. We kept our light sources low, so as to not give away our presence too early. Visibility was reduced to about a dozen feet. Xagrim's conspicuously loud metallic footsteps would probably notify the creature before we even knew where it was.

After what seemed like an eternity, the hallway exited into a massive space. It was impossible to tell how large the room was, but it felt infinite. The thought that some massive reptilian beast's eye could be focusing on us at the moment sent shivers down my spine.

Venturing out a few feet, I called for the group to pause as we listened for any sign of the creature. Nothing.

"Maybe it's sleeping?" Carine whispered.

"Then we shall slay it as it slumbers," Xagrim said. It seemed the knight was looking forward to killing something after being forced to attend the uncanny ball.

We moved farther into the inky darkness, leaving the safety of the hall behind. I couldn't even tell which way we'd just come. The feeling of being exposed out in the open while we could see nothing around us was maddening.

"Prepare for battle. I'm going to illuminate the room," I said as I began focusing on my spell.

"Multae Illuminous Manifestae!" I shouted as I sent eight blinding orbs of light out from our position, racing forth to every corner and wall in the gargantuan room.

"Oh, my gods..." Carine whispered at the sight before us.

It seemed whatever threat the dragon posed had faded long ago. Fifty years? One hundred? It was impossible to say. The beast's skeletal remains curled in front of us, with its head and tail looped around each other, as if the creature had died in hibernation or sleep.

While I had seen pictures of the creatures, this was probably the smallest specimen on record. It looked like it was perhaps one hundred feet from head to tail. While still large when compared to most creatures, dragons of lore were thought to have reached sizes ten times that of this one.

Flaccid, saggy, paper-like skin hung from the monster's bony frame. Its wings were folded in on its back, still attached by decaying ligaments. I wondered if the magical nature of the creature had slowed its decay, or if it was merely a lack of predators and the cool, arid environment of this level's atmosphere.

"At least we won't have to fight it," Carine said with disappointment in her voice.

"Where is the key? We need to get to the Soul Sphere," I said.

Carine moved toward the dragon, checking her scanner as she went. Upon reaching the creature's head, which looked as if it could swallow several gnomes at once, she patted one large tooth. "Inside here, I think."

"Xagrim."

The knight moved past Carine and grasped the creature's upper and lower jaws. Slowly, he pried them apart and held them open. We all looked to the feisty gnome with expectation.

"Inside?" she said meekly.

"You're the smallest," I said.

Grumbling, she shook her head as she lit a torch and crawled in the dragon's maw. "First, I'm a frog, then engulfed in slime, now I have to crawl inside a dragon's mouth...and this isn't even my dungeon..."

"I guarantee I'll find you a ruby," I shouted after her.

"Better be two rubies to compensate for all of this," a muffled voice from inside the dragon's skull complained. "Got it."

"Now we need the door," Zarah said.

Looking around the room and our current position, I pointed toward the dragon's ribcage. "Judging by the layout's similarity to the Dire Hall above, it's going to be there."

Zarah pointed toward the thick bones blocking our path. "How are we going to get through all of that? It's all still connected, and those bones must weigh tons."

"Is this something you can animate, Helatha?" I asked.

The soul snatcher took a step back. "I-I've never attempted anything of this size." My unwavering gaze let her know it wasn't a request. If we couldn't move the dragon or get through the door, the quest was finished. "It will be done, Master. The spell will require extensive preparation, however."

"Good. Let me know if there's anything we can do to assist you. As for the rest of us, I'd like to set up a few traps down the hall leading to this room. Anything to delay or incapacitate the intruders."

"Finally, I can do something!" Carine said as she began shuffling through her bags.

"Do you have any delayed trap-type spells, Gogbog?" I asked. The elderly goblin shook his head in the negative. "No spells."

Helatha started drawing complicated sigils and diagrams around the dragon. It looked as if it would take her at least two hours to complete her work. "Let's go, Carine," I said as we left the group behind.

"These are the same guys who attacked you the first time?" Carine asked.

"I suspect they are. They are powerful enemies, but they also seem to have the ability to mask their presence from the dungeon and even control or incapacitate my minions through some unknown method."

"Think we can stop them?"

"If we don't, the dungeon will die. I suspect the upper levels are already weakening from the loss of magic flowing into them."

"Guess we'll just have to let 'em know who's boss, then, right?" Carine said with a smile.

"Indeed."

WE RETURNED TO THE group an hour later to find Helatha was mostly finished with her spell diagrams. Sweat beaded her forehead as she pushed herself to her limits.

"Forgive me...normally I wouldn't spend less than half a day on such a complicated necromantic spell," she admitted as she poured over a unique pattern of jagged shapes.

"You're doing fine, I can't imagine we will face anyone until —" I began to say before a muffled explosion sounded from far down the tunnel.

"That was one of my gnombot mines," Carine said.

"Already?" Zarah asked.

I took one last sip of the magic potion vial and handed the rest to Helatha. "We need to hold them until she finishes."

For the next twenty minutes, the sound of explosions, fireballs, and other spells and gadgets erupted from the hallway as the interlopers drew closer to our position. We moved about fifty feet away from the exit, ready to attack as soon as the group appeared.

The flashes of fury and explosions grew closer until we could see the images of the approaching troop at a distance. I released a massive fireball at the last position of the group. The spell detonated after traveling down the hall a hundred and fifty feet. An arrow zoomed by my head, missing my helm by what sounded like an inch.

"Dungeon Lord Therion, we've come to eradicate your dungeon in the name of Castigous and Mistress Bitter. You're charged with being weak and unfit to carry out His will. Your Soul Sphere is destroyed. Die," a harsh voice from the shadows announced.

"You'll have to take me," I shouted back.

"You're already taken. You're just not wise enough to realize it yet. Kill them," the voice said as the group dashed from the mouth of the hall. The first member failed to notice one of Carine's gnombots flattened against the dungeon floor. The spider-like device hopped up and ran toward the enemy, exploding in a shower of shrapnel and flame that knocked the warrior back ten feet.

Its familiar robes in tatters, I was surprised to see a massive stone gargoyle scrambling to rise from the ground. It was at least seven feet tall and as wide as a horse. Its long beaked nose split between two glowing yellow eyes. Curled horns similar to a sheep's graced its skull. Underneath its ruined robes, incredibly thick mail armor that looked like it weighed several hundred pounds protected the beast's durable stone body. In its talon-like hands rested a massive cylindrical metal club, ridged with rounded rivets.

The gargoyle shook off the lingering effects of the explosion and began running toward us again as a robed figure in the back unleashed arrow after arrow at Xagrim. Some of the arrows erupted into blazing fire as others crystallized into ice before striking the knight. His left arm caught fire while his left leg began to freeze over with ice as more arrows assaulted him.

Without Toxin, it was up to me to help form a front line of defense with Xagrim as Carine and Gogbog attacked from the rear. Gogbog's first totem crackled with electricity as his second created a shower of water that cleansed the magical fire that had spread to Xagrim's torso and helm. The raincloud moved away from our group to pause in the middle of the battlefield.

Meanwhile, Carine at last had a chance at combat, just as she'd wished. Firing her curious wrist catapult, explosive shots erupted around the charging gargoyle, blackening its armor and exposed stone skin, but doing minimal damage to the incredibly tough juggernaut. She ceased her attack and began pulling parts out of her bags and pouches.

Their second warrior slung its bow across its back and bounded across the field on all fours. Leaping through the air, it landed on the gargoyle's shoulder before a second jump carried it over our heads and behind Xagrim and me.

"Look out!" I cried out as Gogbog attempted to shuffle away from the incredibly acrobatic enemy. The robed menace pulled back one arm to strike, causing its sleeve to slide down, revealing a razor-sharp clawed weapon.

"Oh, no, you don't!" Carine shouted as she stepped away from the gadget she'd assembled in seconds. It resembled a wooden crate with small mead barrels on either side of it. A

long metal tube jutted out from the front of the crate. The entire assembly rested on a tripod. Carine pointed toward the
nimble attacker threatening Gogbog and touched a control
on her gauntlet. The device whirred into motion, firing what
looked like metal balls at the enemy. The first one struck it in
the shoulder, causing the creature to hiss and rear back before
backflipping away from the oncoming projectiles.

"Meet the Defense-O-Matic One Thousand," Carine said
with pride. The turret tracked the movements of the creature,
firing a ball bearing every few seconds until it moved away from
Carine and Gogbog.

"It's a felae!" I shouted over my shoulder as I analyzed the
remaining two members. Zarah had mentioned five, plus the
one above...had one fallen to our traps in the tunnel, or were
we dealing with something that could employ stealth? Perhaps
Zarah would locate it before it could strike — I'd just noticed
the two in the back seemed to be casting spells. The one on the
right flicked her hand toward me. Leaping to the side, I avoided an eruption of scalding steam that shot up from the earth.

I was more concerned about the large one on the left. This
had to be a creature similar to the one that had incapacitated
Xagrim, Zarah, and Toxin from the first attack on the dungeon. It stood immobile, giving the impression of a large body
under its huge robes, but I suspected it was another illusion.

"Ignatous Globulus!" I shouted as I unleashed a small fireball toward the figure. Before the spell could impact, my target
blurred and suddenly there were over fifty identical images of
it throughout the room. The errant fireball exploded on the far
wall.

Before I could move again, a flash of black electricity flashed before my eyes, and I saw nothing but white as I crumpled to the floor. The smell of brimstone and ozone filled the air. My limbs quaked and quivered as I tried to shake off the effects of the spell. The spellcaster on the right pointed again. This time I rolled out of the way as another bolt of midnight-black energy struck the ground beside me.

It was going to be difficult to deal with the true threat while dodging spells. Casting a glance at Xagrim, I found him locked in a battle of titans with the gargoyle. Electricity danced around them both as Gogbog's totem pulsed and sent bolt after bolt toward Xagrim and the water pooled on the floor. The gargoyle jerked and winced slightly with each bolt, while Xagrim's metal body seemed to direct the electricity into his sword, which crashed again and again into the gargoyle's massive club. It seemed the pair were evenly matched, even with Gogbog's elemental assistance.

Gogbog had summoned a spiritual mountain lion that tracked and slashed at the felae warrior's legs and arms if the warrior came too close to Carine and the shaman. Between the turret and the ghostly lion, the felae had little time to aim her bow.

The right figure in the back cast another spell, but this time directed at the gargoyle. The stone colossus grew in size slightly, its armor and weapon increasing in size along with it. It lifted its towering club over its head and brought it down in a double-handed blow that Xagrim elected to step back from. The stone floor cracked as rock shrapnel bounced in every direction. The death knight attempted to block the next few blows, but he was outmatched by the empowered gargoyle. With one explosive smash, Xagrim fell back as his sword slid across the floor toward Carine.

The battle was too chaotic. If any of our party fell, the tide would change instantly. Electing to give Xagrim a breather, I shouted, "Terrem Liquesi!" toward the gargoyle. The heavy creature quickly sank up to its knees in the softened floor. The other caster began casting a spell I suspected would remove my soften ground spell.

The far-right caster shouted, "Attack the Dungeon Master, Setha!"

I whirled to see the felae leaping upon me, slashing in rapid succession with the claw weapon gauntlets it wore. The first strike sliced across my helm, while I blocked the second with my free arm. The nimble cat woman moved with blinding speed, and my armor weighed me down slightly. Only my training with Toxin gave me a chance to counter her moves.

"For a Dungeon Master, you fight well. Most of your kind is content to let others fight their battles," the felae warrior said as she leapt back from my sword swing. Before I could recover, she sprung forward and jammed her right claw weapon in the small opening between my breastplate and right pauldron. The tips of her claws cut through my padding and dug deep into my underarm. She jumped up and wrapped her legs around my outstretched sword arm, locking it into place.

She leaned in and grinned. "I'll saw your arm off underneath your armor."

Swinging my free hand at her, she caught it and held it. Despite my greater strength, I couldn't find leverage to grab her.

"Want to know a secret?" Zarah whispered in the felae warrior's ear as she appeared in the air beside us. "Felae have *really* sensitive hearing." The Dungeon Heart drew a massive breath before unleashing a magically enhanced scream that sent my own ears ringing. The nimble feline warrior released her grip as she grasped the sides of her head in pain and fell to the floor.

Bringing my sword high, I was about to deliver the death blow to the stunned cat warrior before a swarm of sickening insects blackened the air, stinging and biting at my open flesh. The swarm was dispersed by Gogbog's nature magic a moment later, but I could feel the poisons beginning to burn through my veins. Seconds later, a cure poison spell from the elder shaman removed that as well. Meanwhile, the felae had escaped.

The deafening clang of metal on metal to our right revealed Xagrim was barely holding his own against the empowered gargoyle. The felae had retreated to the far side of the room, where the caster of their group waited. I suddenly had a bad feeling about the situation.

Looking around at the dozens of images of the group's mysterious last member revealed a glowing energy field pulsing around it. I launched several flame darts, but they passed harmlessly through illusions.

"Master! I've almost completed the ritual!" Helatha called out from behind.

"Focus on the gargoyle, Carine and Gogbog! Then move back to Helatha's position!" I shouted as I began to cast a spell at the giant stone beast. Xagrim ducked under a crippling swing of the monster's giant club just as several explosive projectiles erupted in its face. Gogbog's spirit cat leapt upon the gargoyle's back, digging its claws into its ring mail armor. The small delayed fireball I'd cast fell at its feet before exploding with enough force to send the creature reeling back a dozen feet.

"How much longer?" I asked the breathless soul snatcher.

"I...need to finish this last diagram, Master."

"Good, once it's completed —" I began to say before a wave of energy washed over the room. Xagrim crashed to the floor as Gogbog struggled to stand. The elder shaman fell back, seemingly in slow motion. Zarah cried out before falling to her knees. Helatha lay unconscious and immobile at my feet.

"Are you all right?" I said as I knelt beside Zarah.

"It's...like the last time. So...weak," she whispered. "Maybe worse."

"What-what happened?" Carine asked as she looked over the devastated remnants of our party. "Is this what you were talking about?"

"It's some ability of the large one that overcomes the dungeon's minions," I said as I analyzed the situation. We'd barely held our own with the full group. Now it was merely the pair of us against the four of them. Casting a wall of fire in the middle of the room, I then liquified the ground on the other side of the gargoyle's current position.

"Do you have any more tricks in your bag that could help us?" I asked.

"Not really. I packed more gear for exploration than going to war. We already used up my mines in the hall, and the turret is almost out of ammunition."

I glanced down at Helatha's handiwork. I'd never seen such a complex reanimation spell, but I'd trained with her enough to understand what the spell was doing.

"Keep them busy," I said as I began finishing the design.

"Keep...all of them busy?" Carine asked.

I attempted to follow the path of magic through the spell's intricate twists and turns. "Indeed. Quietly, if you are able."

"I think I'm going to need more than a ruby for this," the gnome said as she moved her turret away from the group.

As I worked on the confusing and difficult spell, I cast glances to see if Carine needed assistance. The gargoyle rushed through the flames, having recovered from our combined attack, only to fall into the quagmire of liquified stone on the other side. Its immense weight caused it to sink up to its waist instantly. Gogbog's spirit animal had seemingly vanished, either dispelled or destroyed.

The felae leapt over the top of the flames, only to face Carine's ranged attacks. The feline warrior unleashed several arrows of her own, but her aim was off due to constant dodging.

The spell formula was almost complete, but there were several sigils I'd been unsure of. The final spell parameters were beyond anything I'd seen so far, but desperation called for me to finish it with something. The gargoyle had almost extracted itself and would be charging us at any moment.

"The turret's out of ammo! I'm going to — agh!" Carine shouted as she caught an arrow in her arm. She staggered back, a look of shock on her face as if she didn't know what to do next. It must have been the first time she'd actually been seriously injured in combat.

"I'm done," I said as I unleashed a barrage of flame and ice darts at the felae and gargoyle. My flame wall died instantly, apparently dispelled by the mysterious caster on the far side of the room.

Carine's eyes grew wider as she looked past me. Turning, I saw the skull of the deceased dragon rising from the floor, two glowing green embers now inhabiting its empty eye sockets. Like a snake rising to strike, the rest of the neck moved upward until the body began to tremble. The skeletal dragon's legs clicked together and slammed to the ground as its wings unfurled. The beast's tail swished back and forth as if the creature were agitated. Its whole body shook, sloughing off bits of scaled skin and dust.

The felae backed away as the gargoyle paused to regard the new enemy. Unlike a golem or other animated stone creature, a gargoyle possessed sentience and understood danger and threats.

Carine fell on her behind as a terrifying roar escaped the creature's nonexistent throat. The ghostly, shrill sound wasn't one I would have expected from a dragon.

The creature took a step forward before it noticed the small beings gathered around its feet. Its glowing eyes first regarded the gargoyle, then the felae, then our party, which was scattered closest to it.

"It is under your control, right?" Carine asked as she clambered to her feet and made her way to my side.

"I believe so —" I said before the dragon reared back. "Unless I got that one sigil wrong..."

"Die!" the undead dragon hissed as it unleashed a torrent of black flame at us.

CHAPTER TWENTY
Master

Leaping to the side, I tackled Carine, carrying us both away from the necromantic fire. The crackling black flames missed the rest of the party, except for Xagrim's sprawled legs. I couldn't tell what effect they'd had on the death knight. An arrow clanged into my back, the icy cold beginning to spread. Nullifying the enchantment with a dispel magic spell prevented any frostbite, but the chill reached into my very bones.

"What do we do?" Carine asked as the dragon roared again. For now, the gargoyle and felae warrior were keeping their distance, while the enemy spellcaster waited to see how the situation would progress.

I looked around frantically for a solution. We were caught between two powerful enemies, and our allies were vulnerable. That's when I noticed the exposed door to the next room.

"Here, let's trade," Carine said as she shoved the key into my hand and took my shield. She pulled out a pair of dark goggles. "Welding goggles. You got enough magic for those blinding orbs?"

"Yes, I've still a fair amount of magic. What are you planning?"

Now dashing toward the gargoyle and felae, the gnome engineer shouted, "Let 'em rip!"

"What are you doing?" I shouted after her.

She turned to fire several explosive shells into the dragon's skull, causing it to roar in anger. It turned its attention to the fleeing gnome and began moving slowly after her. Ducking, I barely managed to avoid the huge tail as it swished overhead.

Carine ducked and bobbed as the felae and enemy caster realized what the gnome was doing and fired arrows and several spells at the gnome. The shield I'd given her blocked several of the projectiles while the nimble small gnome proved to be a difficult target. The dragon was gaining speed as life seemed to flow into its ancient limbs and it remembered how to move.

"Multae Subtemporus Illuminous Manifestae!" I shouted as I summoned forth two small dots of light and sent them flying to the spot where Carine would be in several seconds. I then ran toward the massive door the dragon's prone body had been blocking.

A blinding flash from behind engulfed the room in more light than a hundred sunrises. Even with my eyes closed and facing the opposite direction, I saw spots. The roar of the dragon and cries from the enemy group signaled the spell had worked well. Upon reaching the door, I fumbled with the key until it was unlocked. Flinging it open, I was surprised to see another throne room. This one dwarfed my current throne room and appeared to be ripped straight from a castle that was much larger than the castle in New Vadis. Just as the ballroom above, this area looked immaculately maintained.

Ignoring the illustrious decor, I scanned the room for the Soul Sphere. There, on the far side of the room, a large throne rested atop a dais. It gleamed as if made of gold or silver, but it was the color of blood. The striated surface reminded me of exposed muscle tissue. Black padding covered the seat and backrest, while two arms rose up from each side of the back of the throne, twisting together into a spiral that grew up to house the darkened Soul Sphere. The metal at the base of the sphere crawled up around the orb, looking like sickly roots holding it fast. The sphere itself was at least double the size of the one above.

Dashing forward, I was suddenly struck from behind as the felae fell upon me with a kick that sent me sprawling. The roars and shouts from outside indicated her compatriots were still preoccupied with the dragon. I hoped Carine had managed to find safety.

"So close," the cat warrior said as she leapt high into the air. I rolled to the side just as both of her feet came down where my head had been a moment earlier. I attempted to sweep her legs out from under her, but she flipped away. Scrambling to my feet, I attacked. She easily ducked and dodged several swings from Purgatory before blocking one with the back of her gauntlet.

Her robe's hood now fell away; I could see the cat woman's gleaming golden fur that was laced with rows of brown stripes. Her long, brown hair cascaded just past her shoulders, with two feline ears poking through the sides.

Reversing her hand, she held my blade in a strong grip. "It's over. The Interferous has shut down your minions, and the dragon will be dealt with shortly."

"Interferous? Is that what the floating head creatures are called? The ones that you use to control the dungeon's minions?"

She smiled, flashing her fangs. "Why resist? You could perhaps even join us, if Askith permits it. Mistress Bitter is very merciful to those who prove useful. You're a powerful warrior and magic user, and you have a reputation as a scholar. Just surrender and return with us."

"What would happen to Zarah and the others if I were to do so?" I asked.

She laughed. "A dungeon needs but one heart, and your minions are too weak to be of use to someone like Mistress Bitter. Your dungeon would collapse, and you'd forfeit your kingdom."

"I'll have to decline, then," I said as I ripped my sword free from her grasp. She jerked in surprise as she looked at the blood drawn from her palm.

"You're strong — and dangerous," she said as she backed away.

I glanced over my shoulder toward the Soul Sphere. If I could just reach it...

A whirling sound turned my attention back to the felae. She held a bladed claw weapon in her hand and twirled the other one on the end of a chain. It was similar to the one Zarah and I had found, except this one had claw sickles on both ends of the chain.

She whirled the weapon faster and faster, changing direction with it so that it wound around her body. Twirling with it, she danced about until both ends were a blur. Before I could react, one of the ends rushed past my head. I ducked just as she jerked it back, causing the now scythe-like curved end to glance off the back of my helm instead of plunging into my neck.

"Oh, you're aware of how a tor-serre works? I'm surprised," she teased. "That's because most people die before they can figure it out." She whirled both ends of the weapon even faster, flicking them both at me at the same time.

"Stop," a voice from the doorway shouted. The felae grimaced, but did as she was ordered, recalling the weapon and storing it.

"Your dragon is defeated, as is this...annoyance," the speaker said before tossing Carine's body to the floor. From this distance, I couldn't tell if she was unconscious or dead.

The gargoyle stood behind her as the mysterious floating entity hid behind him.

"You should surrender, and Mistress Bitter may find use for you, Master Therion. It may seem like a humiliating defeat, but this is a generous offer. It seems she is most impressed with your performance since taking over this dungeon from Orgun."

"And you are...Askith?" I said.

The robed figured turned her head toward the felae warrior. "I see you couldn't resist divulging our secrets, Setha. Mistress Bitter may take your tongue again if you aren't careful. Yes, I am Askith, this is Setha, and our large friend here is Bassault."

"Your silent member is Interferous?" I asked.

"It is *an* Interferous, yes, but its designation is Collective Eight. I'm not sure how you managed to best our scouting party, but this Interferous is much stronger than the one you first dealt with, as you've experienced yourself. None may resist Mistress Bitter's willpower when relayed through an Interferous of this magnitude. Now, I have to beg the question — what do we do with you? You could join us and live out the rest of your life as a privileged servant of Mistress Bitter, or we could simply kill you here. We were instructed to take you alive, if possible. You're a man of reason and knowledge, so surely you can see your position. I'd prefer not to harm you further."

I glanced over my shoulder at the Soul Sphere. Even if I could reach it, what then? I had no magic to fill it. It would serve no strategic benefit at the moment. But something inside told me I needed to activate it, no matter what.

"I see you are still entertaining the idea of resisting us. Once your heart is destroyed, you'll have no option. Bring her forth," she ordered. The hovering member to the rear floated forward, at last revealing Zarah's unconscious form held in a long, slender tentacle. I was surprised it could touch her ethereal form.

"No! Leave her be! I'll come with you if you don't harm her," I shouted.

"Our orders were to destroy this dungeon. The scouting party failed twice so far, which is why *we* were dispatched this time. Failure means eternal agony," she said as she motioned toward Collective Eight. Another tentacle unrolled from the creature's underside and stabbed into Zarah's chest. She awoke for a moment and gasped before falling still.

The intense pain in my own chest was unlike anything I'd felt before. It was similar to when the Soul Sphere above had shattered, but more intense. Falling to my knees, I couldn't breathe. A crushing weight squeezed my lungs as I tried to draw air.

"You'll need to attune yourself to our orb or you'll die, Master Therion," Askith said as she revealed another of the portable spheres.

The pain was unbearable. Was Zarah gone? Was she dying? I could barely see her through the red haze of my pain.

"Bring him here," Askith ordered. "Quickly, before he passes."

The felae warrior kicked Purgatory away before scooping my powerless body up into her arms. I stared at Zarah's fading spirit as I drew closer. Had I failed her again? Memories flashed back to when Xagrim had killed Zarah's human form, as the light faded from her eyes. I thought of the threats from Inevitable Oblivion, when Kys nearly destroyed us all. The look of Zarah's pleading eyes as Leath had threatened to take me out of the dungeon.

There had to be something I could do. Did Xagrim, Helatha, and Gogbog still live, or had they been eliminated while I fought Setha? Could I reactivate them somehow, as I had done when I pulled Zarah's spirit through the ether from the broken Soul Sphere to the portable one I held?

Reaching out my will, I attempted to feel for my minions. Perhaps I could awaken them or overcome this ability that overrode my willpower with that of Mistress Bitter's control. I was surprised to feel instead other tethers in the air, closer. Foreign links to an alien, yet familiar magic. Minions closer than my own.

Askith, Bassault, and Setha seemed bound to the willpower of Collective Eight, not the portable sphere. Probing deeper, it seemed the sphere provided the magic for their survival, but the will of their master emanated from the Interferous. Just as my minions needed my force of will to function, as well as a pool of magic provided from the Soul Sphere and Zarah, these invaders depended on both the creature and the orb to exist outside of their own lair. That was how they were over-riding the dungeon. The Interferous was designed to block the willpower of the dungeon's master...causing minions to weaken, flee in fear, or fail to notice the intruders. Mistress Bitter's will pushed mine away and allowed Askith to issue commands to my dungeon through Collective Eight.

The weakness...was my own. I'd allowed these beings to control my dungeon — my minions. My will had proved insufficient and easily dismissed by another Master, even at a distance. I had no idea where this Mistress Bitter was, but she'd crushed my dungeon's spirit without even showing herself in person.

No! I wouldn't allow it. I had worked so hard to rebuild this dungeon. I had sacrificed my own freedom, paid for its success with my own blood and sweat. My minions looked to me for leadership. New Vadis and the dungeon would collapse without my guidance. I would not allow my dungeon to fall to these interlopers!

Setha must have sensed something had changed as she looked down at me with concern. "What are you —" she said before my hand grabbed her exposed wrist. I reached deep inside the warrior cat woman, finding another presence there — the willpower of the enemy, Mistress Bitter. My anger growing, I pushed my own will into this vessel, feeling the control of the other draining away. I envisioned a corpse with its neck slit and held upside down, its blood draining onto the floor. Another image flashed...that of the symbol of Castigous. My rage and thoughts flooded Setha's spiritual form, filling her with my will.

"What..." the felae warrior said as she fell under my control. I willed her to continue carrying me toward her party. Setting me down near Collective Eight, Setha backed away.

"First, allow the Interferous to draw your tainted magic from your body. Do not fight it. Then I will synchronize you to our sphere," Askith explained.

The large floating member of the group moved above me as a tentacle snaked out, tentatively probing areas of my body as if determining how to proceed. It then jerked back, alarmed by something, and whirled to face Askith, apparently communicating with her telepathically or through some similar method.

"What?" the spellcaster asked as she turned to regard Setha. It seemed the unusual creature had detected my ruse.

"Wait...I haven't given you my magic yet," I said as I opened my palm, revealing a small delayed fireball orb. The spell struck the floating creature in its vulnerable underside, sending its mass of tentacles writhing. Its cloak and illusion fell away simultaneously, revealing what appeared to be a shrunken giant's head. Its mouth had been sewn shut, and its exposed brain pulsed as it grunted and reeled from my assault, flames and smoke trailing it.

At the same time, Setha slashed across Askith's face, knocking back her hood, revealing an ashen elf with long gray hair and black, soulless eyes. The same twin nodules rested upon her brow that all other minions of Mistress Bitter seemed to possess.

Bassault appeared confused by the situation unfolding. His group members were attacking each other, while Collective

Eight's pain had caused the disembodied head to emit conflicting commands or emotions in the stone minion.

I rolled away and struggled to rise to my feet as I hobbled toward the Soul Sphere. The pain in my chest was stronger than ever, but I ignored the thundering in my ears as I focused solely on reaching the orb. Other than that singular goal, the world faded around me. No...I was blacking out. I reached into the pouch on my belt and pulled out our portable orb...it was nearly empty. I didn't have enough magic to bring anyone back.

"Stop him, you fool!" Askith shouted. The thundering footsteps of the gargoyle began following me, but I'd nearly reached the orb. I could feel the beast bearing down on me, and I imagined that massive club flattening me to paste, but I ignored it and reached out toward the dead sphere just ahead. *Just another few feet...don't think about anything but the sphere.* Just as it felt as if the stone monstrosity would stamp me flat — contact.

The sphere glowed with life as I felt the energy of the lower half of the dungeon flow into me. The sewer level, the psuthals, the puzzle level, the knights...we connected as if a gate had opened and water began to pour forth from a dam. But not just the new levels...I once again felt Ho'Scar, the skeletons, the arbolisks, the goblins, and the rest of the dungeon once again. It was as if I'd been made whole after losing my limbs. Then I felt another presence. One that offered assistance in my time of need. I beckoned it, *"Come."*

The pain in my chest decreased as I felt a new confidence and strength flow into my body. Diving to the side, I barely managed to avoid the gargoyle's massive club that caused half of the throne to crumble with one blow. Casting a glance to the far end of the throne room revealed Askith monitoring the battle, while Setha's immobile form had been imprisoned in a block of ice. Collective Eight seemed agitated, but the flames had died away or had been dispelled. I hadn't expected the spell to kill it, but I'd hoped it would at least have been crippled by the attack.

"I've never seen a dungeon master overcome one of us with his own willpower. You must have a strong will, indeed, if you can override the Interferous," Askith said. "But even with the Soul Sphere reactivated, you'll die without your dungeon heart," the elf said as she gestured to the spot where Zarah had fallen. It was now empty.

I motioned to the floor beside the throne. "She's with me now. You won't harm her again."

"Please don't make us destroy you. See reason. You're unarmed and outmatched. Serving Mistress Bitter is a better fate than spending eternity facing Castigous' torture for failing him. Surely you realize this?" Askith asked. "Don't let the folly of youth cloud your reason and judgment."

"*You* should surrender. Best to face my torture chamber than Castigous' wrath, correct?" I said. "Work for me instead of your current master. My minions would tell you they are well taken care of."

"Your minions are defeated and defenseless against us. You're an inexperienced whelp, powerless to stop us. Take him by force," Askith said.

The gargoyle resumed his attack, reaching for me with his massive stone hand. With one swift motion, I sent the creature's severed hand flying through the air and tumbling down the stairs, where it crumbled to bits. The beast howled and reared back before raising its massive club over its head. I readied the invisible sword for a second strike.

"No! Do not kill him!" Askith shouted in panic as the club fell.

The surge of power I felt after connecting to the new Soul Sphere continued to rise. It felt similar to the unknown rage that had filled me when my father groveled at my feet for mercy. It was time to administer punishment to these invaders. This was my dungeon. They presumed to defeat me in my own home? This, I could not allow.

The club came crashing down but stopped instantly as my raised hand intercepted it. My gauntlet buckled as the straps on my arm's armor snapped. The gargoyle looked at its weapon in confusion. Marveling at my exposed, well-muscled arm, I laughed.

"How...?" Askith asked.

"Unlike your Mistress Bitter, I fight my own battles. I've trained and sacrificed for my power. While my minions assist me, I fight with them. I killed the Strong One. I solved the puzzles. I defeated the knights as well as the king slime. Without a Soul Sphere to fuel, where do you think all that powerful energy went? I took it within myself."

Askith's calm demeanor faded into one of fear. "Kill him!"

With one swift motion, I jerked the club from the gargoyle's grasp and flipped it around before ramming it into the creature's midsection, leaving a gaping crater at the center of the beast. The mail armor provided no protection from the blunt weapon's shattering impact. The monster stumbled backward, but it didn't seem to be a mortal wound.

"Subtemporus Rhymeous Globulus," I whispered as I opened my palm toward the wound. A small bluish-white sphere glided toward the center of the gargoyle before coming to rest. Backing away, I turned before the spell activated.

The stone beast attempted to grab the orb right as it exploded, creating a massive ball of ice that shattered into a rain of ice shards. The gargoyle crumbled into pieces as the ice expanded within the wound and blew it apart.

A bolt of mental energy slammed into my psyche before I could move. A vision of blood, rage, fear, pain. Bodies ripped and split apart, black clouds of decay and poison. Chains, spikes, blades, and worse assaulted my senses. I felt my willpower falter. An image of a sultry silhouette dancing inside a deluge of blood raining from the sky. Glowing green eyes within the darkness. This was the will of Mistress Bitter. I wanted to murder and love her at the same time. Worship and cower, flee and embrace. The conflicting emotions blurred the world around me, but I could tell they were emanating from Collective Eight. Askith had begun casting a spell while I battled the creature's concentrated willpower.

Reaching out, I let my own willpower flow through the lower levels of the dungeon and searched. It was here.

A shower of glowing blue blood exploded from Collective Eight, covering Askith with the vile and putrid liquids. A pity...I'd hoped to save it for dissection later, but its mental assault had proved too dangerous to ignore. Askith sputtered and spat as the dark liquids sprayed her face, interrupting her spell.

Collective Eight spasmed and jerked as it fell to the floor, a perfect hole driven through the center of its forehead.

Askith looked to me in surprise. Orgun's staff levitated horizontally before me, blood dripping and dotting the dry, stone floor beneath it. I reached out and grasped it in my unarmored fist. It seemed to be pleased with the situation, as its touch warmed my bare flesh.

"You've done well. We can work with this."

Another bolt of black lightning erupted from above, but instead of arcing through my body, it traveled into the staff and dissipated.

"Now...as you were saying?" I said as I took a step toward Askith.

She looked at the remains of the floating giant's head, the frozen felae, and the pieces of the gargoyle before darting out of the room.

"Kill her," the staff ordered. *"I need more."*

"No," I said as I turned and raced to Zarah's side. Upon first glance, I thought she was gone, due to how faint she'd become during the fight. She hadn't moved at all since I'd summoned her across the room.

I looked at the Soul Sphere, which was now perhaps five percent full, due to the deaths of the gargoyle and the Interferous.

"Zarah," I said as I focused my will upon her prone form. Nothing happened.

"You do not possess enough magic to repair the Dungeon Heart in your weakened state."

"Then I will kill Askith," I said as I turned to track down the fleeing caster.

"You will need much more than that. It will not be enough."

"Much more...?" I whispered as I watched Zarah slowly fading. "Then we will gather it all."

Ho'Scar jumped as I appeared beside him. "Master! Where'd ya come from? I was just loadin' up all the prisoners! I didn't know what the hells had happened when that shock went through the dungeon. Felt like we was dyin' or somethin', but felt right good all of a sudden about half an hour ago. I figured I'd get the prisoners going again, so as to fill up yer sphere."

"There is no time for explanation," I said as I let my will spread throughout the room. There were fifteen prisoners in various torture devices. I reached out with my open hand and focused.

"What...what are you doin', Master? Can I help you?"

"Silence," I said as I connected to each machine and felt the bodies writhing inside. I took in their fear, their hatred, their pain. Slowly, I closed my hand as I exerted my dominance over the very physical material of the dungeon.

Levers moved down as cranks began to turn. Fires burned hotter and wood constricted around arms and necks. Spikes grew into the flesh of their victims as hot oils flamed. The moans of the tortured turned into screams of pain and panic.

"Very good," the staff whispered.

As my hand closed into a fist, the symphony of death ceased. I felt the life force of the prisoners flow into the dungeon, feeding it.

"By the gods..." Ho'Scar said as I disappeared.

In seconds, I reappeared in the throne room on level thirteen. Casting a glance at the Soul Sphere, I noticed it was now twenty five percent full. I prayed it was enough. Releasing the staff, I focused my will on Zarah.

"Return to me, Zarah. I order you to obey," I said. She did not respond.

"Why isn't it working?" I asked as I fell to my knees beside her and leaned over the fallen Dungeon Heart.

She looked as if she were sleeping. The memory of her sleeping contently during our first adventure through the dungeon appeared in my mind. At the time, it had seemed like a nightmare, but now I recalled it with fondness. I'd wanted to hold her close on those terrifying nights as the two of us made our way through the dungeon. She'd later told me she desired the same thing but didn't want me to become too attached to her, for fear I'd do something stupid like sacrifice myself. Yet now, I felt as if I'd failed her, again. Unable to protect my dungeon, its minions, or her.

I reached down instinctively to move a fallen strand of midnight-black hair from her face and felt foolish as I realized it was a useless gesture. Yet...her hair moved. Touching her again, I felt a partial resistance to my finger.

"Zarah!" I said as I gently prodded her. She didn't stir. Where was she fading away to? To Castigous' realm? Would she be tortured for eternity for failing the God of Torture, as Askith had said?

"No," I whispered as I scooped up her body and held her close. I wouldn't let her go. I didn't care about the welfare of the dungeon or myself, but she'd faced so much pain in life, I wouldn't allow her to be punished any more.

The familiar power swirled around me as I hugged her tighter. Her head tilted back limply as her plump lips parted slightly, revealing her fangs. I recalled the songs she'd sing to me as I tried to sleep on troubled nights, her sarcastic jokes as

I worked through difficult situations. Her human and demonic forms, both beautiful in different ways.

Leaning in, I pressed my lips to hers and was surprised as I felt her lips embrace mine. I closed my eyes as I hugged her tighter, and I poured myself into the kiss. I wanted to fill her body with my strength, my soul. The magic of the dungeon. My willpower and all that I was. She was the Dungeon Heart, but she was also part of *my* heart. Just as the dungeon couldn't exist without her, neither could I. The power grew stronger as I reached out with everything I was and gave it to her. My own pool of magic as the dungeon's master had grown considerably.

Her arms rose up and embraced me as her lips pressed back against mine. I opened my eyes to find her dark eyes regarding me with curiosity, amusement, and...something else.

"Well...this is an interesting development," she whispered as she drew back.

"I thought I'd lost you."

"I felt...like I was floating away. Torn between wanting to be here and the draw of some other place. A place..." she said as a look of fear came over her.

"As long as I'm here, you'll never go there. I'm sorry I failed you again," I said.

"You've never failed me, Mast — Jagen," she said.

"Congratulations on reviving your Dungeon Heart, but you still have a dangerous enemy within your dungeon," Orgun's staff said.

I looked at the Soul Sphere, which still held a decent amount of magic. I'd apparently used mostly my own power to revive Zarah.

"Show me where the intruder is," I said.

Zarah brought up an image of the level above. Askith frantically dashed through the floor that contained the ballroom and approached the door that led up to the sewer level. She paused in the landing room to cast a spell of protection upon herself to ward off the poisonous fumes.

"Toxin," I whispered as I focused the dungeon's magic.

The form under the sheet behind Askith began to stir.

CHAPTER TWENTY-ONE
Aftermath

Zarah's vision of the dungeon zoomed through the levels until it fell upon a body resting upon the walkway above the slime river. A dozen slimes crawled over the exposed upper half of a large ogre. The lower half of the creature had long since been devoured in the caustic river.

"That was the invader that you spoke of?" I asked.

"Yes, that's the one that stayed behind to smash the sphere."

"And we found the remains of the other member of their group in the hall to the second Dire Hall, apparently blown apart by our traps," I said.

Zarah materialized a lute and began to strum it. "What was that creature? It looked like it was part insect. Maybe a friend of yours?" she said as Duke Merromont appeared on top of her lute and scuttled around the instrument.

"There wasn't enough left of it to make a guess. You've found no other invaders in the dungeon?"

"Nope. I think that was the last of them."

"And what about my rubies?" Carine asked as she entered the new throne room.

I nodded toward a long table near the entrance. "The small casket, there."

Upon opening the container, the gnome whistled. "Ten? That's a lot more than we agreed upon."

"Your services were invaluable to the success of our quest. The sack beside it is yours, as well."

She cast a suspicious glance at me before picking up the fairly large sack and shaking it. "Is this gold?"

"Indeed."

"What's this for? You trying to bribe me?"

"In a way. I'd like for you to assist me with some of the...studies I plan to undertake."

"You're going to take *her* into the sanctum?" Zarah asked. She sounded somewhat offended.

"I don't know what would happen if you went into that place. There are magics that open the mind and senses, and they can be addictive. In addition to Orgun's staff, I'd like to have a second person to keep me grounded in reality."

"If it means you don't become lost to that place for weeks at a time, take as many people as you want," Zarah said.

"No, the fewer the better. The knowledge contained inside is invaluable. In the wrong hands, it could be dangerous."

"Invaluable? Then count me in!" Carine said.

"I'll have you sign a confidentiality agreement."

"That's...not fair!" the gnome argued.

"Take it or leave it."

"Fine."

A roar interrupted our conversation.

"You're sure you want to keep that thing around? It's going to take a lot of magic to maintain."

"This level needs protection. What better protection than a dragon?"

"That thing looked like it wanted to snatch me up when I walked by it," Carine said. "If it wasn't on a chain, I wouldn't have come down here."

"Oh, it does want to eat you," Helatha said as she floated through the floor. "The dragonlich doesn't have a fully formed mind, so it wishes to destroy anyone other than the Master." She turned to face me. "It's impressive how quickly you dominated the beast, Master."

I nodded. "I feel as if my strength has grown since we expanded the dungeon."

"I feel it as well...as if we've achieved a new tier," Helatha agreed.

"Maybe it's because of the larger Soul Sphere?" Zarah asked.

"No...the Master's power is growing, and ours grows with it. He's advancing quickly."

"The soul snatcher is correct. You've come very far in a short period of time. You're ready to glimpse the knowledge Orgun has amassed. There is hope for you, yet, fledgling dungeon lord. You should begin your studies as soon as possible," the staff in my lap whispered mentally. It seemed our bond had increased since the attack on the dungeon.

"I still have business to attend to. My duties do not lie with the dungeon alone," I replied mentally to the persistent staff.

I thought back to my visit to the goblin village earlier in the morning. Several guards had been killed when the intruders had attacked, but the invaders had decided to slip through silently without risking a fight with the entire village. How had the intruders known where the teleporter stone had been? It was a security issue we'd have to address as soon as possible.

"What will you do now?" Carine asked.

"I'll study the remains of the two Interferous to understand how they function, then we will see what knowledge Askith possesses about this Mistress Bitter," I replied. "Perhaps Orgun has some notes concerning the subject."

"You should get some rest. You've done as much as you can for today," Zarah suggested.

The thought of a good night's rest in my own bed sounded marvelous. The insanity of the past few days had caught up to me, and the dungeon was safe. I bid everyone good night and teleported to my quarters in the old throne room. The act of moving myself through the dungeon had become second nature and now used much less magic than it had when I'd first attempted it.

After a meal consisting of a massive steak and seasoned vegetables prepared especially by Ho'Scar in celebration of our victory, I showered and selected a new book to read from a pile Ligglethorp had left on my desk. I was surprised to find that the goblin chieftain and I shared similar tastes when it came to books of adventure. For tonight, I would put all worries about the dungeon, the city, and invaders out of my mind and relax to the fullest extent of my ability.

I dimmed the lights and climbed into my kingly bed, burrowing deep in the covers. Approximately five pages into my book, I found sleep to be too powerful of an opponent and drifted off.

Jerking awake, I again felt another presence in my room. Had there been another member of the last party that we'd missed? I mentally cursed when I realized I'd left Purgatory near the shower. Slowly, I began to slip out of bed before I realized there was someone else moving beside me, under the covers. Now, I was angry.

"Helatha, I made myself perfectly clear the last time —" I began to say before two arms pulled me close and I found myself kissing the unknown intruder. Unlike Helatha's cold touch, the warmth of this body brought back memories of Aiyla.

"Who?" I asked as I began to pull away, but a tail wrapped around my waist.

"You know who it is," Zarah whispered.

"But...I thought..."

"I said I never wanted to go back to my human body, but now that you can touch me in this form...I see no reason to resist any longer," she said as she kissed my neck and ran her clawed fingers across my chest.

I tried to think of a reason to protest, but as I stared into her eyes under the dim lights, and her lips pulled back into a devilish grin, I gave up and pulled her close.

"Now, let me show you a type of music I haven't shown anyone in a very long while," my Dungeon Heart whispered as the lights winked out.

Author's Notes:

Please leave a review!

Indie authors can only keep publishing with the support of readers!

Join the Mailing List[1]

(Book release dates, exclusive deals, free book)

Contact/Follow[2]

Other Books by S Mays:

https://www.s-mays.com/the-good-stuff.html

Made in the USA
Monee, IL
07 August 2021

75187533R00143